A "Cozy" Airport Read

Leanne Alyse

Trigger Warnings

This book is not appropriate for anyone under the age of eighteen! Reader discretion is advised.

If you would like to go in blind you can stop reading here. This is a dark rom com, with that comes discussion of sensitive topics as well as physical violence. Below is a list of trigger warnings as well as things to know about the book. I do not condone these characters' actions.

Trigger Warnings: poor representations of BDSM, non con/dub con, murder, kidnapping, drugging, stalking, breath play, gun play, knife play, degradation, turbulence, stockholm syndrome, discussion of and close call with SA (not between main characters)

This book is a work of fiction and not based off real events. Any resemblance to people or events in real life is purely coincidental. Nor is this book meant to be an accurate representation of the real world. This is a fictional story, suspension of disbelief is recommended before opening the pages.

If you have any questions you can reach out to my email: <u>LeanneAlyseAuthor@gmail.com</u>

Your mental health matters <3

To all the readers who dream of getting kidnapped by a book boyfriend who
makes you coffee and calls you a good
girl when you cum on his fingers

Playlist

First Class – Jack Harlow
Devil Doesn't Bargain – Alec Benjamin
Bad for Business – Sabrina Carpenter
my strange addiction – Billie Eilish
Ferrari – Bebe Rexha
Guilty Pleasure – Chappell Roan
Too Sweet – Hozier
Bad Habits – Ed Sheeran
Dancing With Our Hands Tied – Taylor Swift
GUY.exe – Superfruit
I Wanna Be Yours – Arctic Monkeys
Close To You – Gracie Abrams
Bed Chem – Sabrina Carpenter
Amore – Bebe Rexha (ft. Rick Ross)
Paris – The Chainsmokers
Dirty Thoughts – Chloe Adams
Heaven – Julia Michaels
Mastermind – Taylor Swift

Chapter One

Liam

People get too comfortable at airports. They assume with all the massive amounts of security there are no work arounds. Those people are fools.

Although, I don't love thinking of Riley as a fool. What she is, is naive. After all, she hasn't noticed me once following her to or from the bar she likes to write at over the past three months and I don't exactly fit in with a crowd.

My tattoos are particularly noticeable, and it doesn't help for being covert that I am six, five. Hard to hide in a pack when you're so much taller than everyone fucking else. Luckily most of my responsibilities are handled from behind a computer screen and other people do the dirty work, at least most days.

Typically Gabriel and his men handle anything that requires boots on the ground. My childhood friend knows that I am particularly antisocial so he doesn't usually give me anything that requires me to speak to anyone.

I keep my distance from Riley as she heads towards the TSA checkpoint. If someone notices her missing later and checks the TSA records to see who was in front of her and behind her when she came in, my name won't be on it.

Well, my name won't be on the list at all, but rather Daniel Blakely's. One of the many fake IDs I have, but the only one I have on me right now. Getting caught with multiple fake IDs *and* trying to kidnap a woman is a sure fire way to end up in jail. One or the other is easy enough to fain innocence on, but not both. Which is also why I'm not carrying any sort of weapons on me either. Besides, weapons won't make it past TSA.

No, the only thing I have is a bottle of "sertraline" that definitely is not actually sertraline, but the fake label matches the description of the pills inside so no one but me will know that. Unless some random TSA security guard just so happens to look in the bottle and know what actual sertraline looks like, although I seriously doubt that anyone will check.

I watch as Riley shoulders off her backpack, smiling softly at the security guard who is rather rudely telling her to take off her shoes and place them in one of the bins. She just does as instructed though ignoring the aggression that is being directed at her for no fucking reason.

Riley tosses some of her long softly curled honey blonde hair over her shoulder as she moves into the line of people preparing to go through the scanner. Her hazel eyes watch attentively through her glasses the people in front of her, waiting for her turn.

Her outfit is comfortable, a pair of leggings with a nicer looking green flannel over her elegant black tank top so if she takes any selfies for socials she will look presentable from the waist up. She has a large following and maintaining it means daily posts, which is nice for me because keeping tabs on someone who is chronically online is insanely easy.

I stop staring down at my phone, flipping through my email with the ticket confirmation repeatedly as a stall incase someone asks me what I'm doing. The line into TSA has enough space between me and Riley that I should be fine to go through now.

Filing in behind the older couple touching each other in rather surprising ways for two graying people of their age, I ready my ticket and fake ID. The older couple keeps pausing and I'm rather annoyed because Riley had just finished going through TSA which means she is slipping off further into the airport before I'm able to catch up.

I know she will for a while, but the longer the people in front of me spend taking just a few steps forwards the longer it will take for me to catch up to her.

Whatever.

Luckily Riley is always several hours early to the airport so I will have time on the back end while she waits for boarding on the flight she was planning to take. The plane she *will* be taking doesn't leave for another four hours.

The older couple finally works through the line and I come up to the officer with the sour face. Is everyone at this fucking airport chronically in a bad mood?

"ID." The woman says dryly, holding her hand out.

I go to give it to her along with the ticket.

She pushes the ticket back at me. "I don't need that." She hisses. "Stand in front of the camera."

I position myself in frame, having to take a step backwards so my head is actually in the picture. My black hair looks grainy in the crappy camera and my usually perfectly tan skin looks ashen and washed out under the harsh fluorescent lighting. My beard is way thicker than my usual scruff, but that will be gone by this time tomorrow. I only grew it so if I got spotted I would look less like myself.

The officer feeds the ID through the reader. I'm not worried about it though. It is a damned good fake, to the point where the name Daniel Blakely can be found in any database he is searched in. He is more or less a real person, just I'm not him.

She hands the ID back to me and nods, dismissing me to go join the other people in line for the body scanner.

I move along, not really wanting to prolong my encounters with any of these people, it's important that I stay unmemorable. I pull off my backpack then toss it onto the conveyor belt.

"Sir." The man on the other side of the conveyor belt huffs, his voice clearly full of frustration. "You have to put that in a bin." He says, like it is the most obvious thing in the world and I'm a gigantic idiot. I haven't flown commercial since I was like sixteen, I don't fucking remember any of this shit.

I just nod and toss the backpack into one of the trays, before taking off my boots and packing them in next to the backpack.

The guard pulls the bin towards himself and rearranges my stuff since apparently I hadn't done so sufficiently, before pushing it towards the machine and waving me away.

I start to get in line but am stopped when the man standing in front of the scanner says gruffly. "Do you have something on under that hoodie?" I pull the black hoodie over my head before he has to tell me to, undoubtedly ruffling my hair in the process, leaving me in my light blue t-shirt.

The man shoes me out of line to go back to the man with the bins. The other man scowls at me as he grabs my bin with the backpack and throws my hoodie haphazardly on top of it since apparently the neat stacking *doesn't* matter that much.

I get back to the line and see the older couple already on the other side collecting their shit. What is it about being a white guy with tattoos in your thirties that makes airport officials hate you?

After waiting for about five people in front of me I finally get my turn to go through the scanner. "Hands up." The woman on the other side says.

I do as instructed.

"Step out." She waves me towards her. There is a pause and I look over to see the scanner go green. "You're good. Step in." She says, already turning her attention to the next person.

I grab my crap the second it comes through the machine, nothing was even flagged so I am able to just toss everything back on and start to look for Riley.

She has a routine. Every time she leaves out of this airport she stops at the Starbucks nearest her gate to get herself whatever seasonal beverage is available. She will take an aesthetically pleasing photo of it in front of her window seat for her Instagram since her followers love to see it. It is her little prelude to let them know she is going away somewhere on a workcation.

Her readers are always thrilled because most of the time a vacation means a novella will be coming out that she will speed write during her trip. They take to her comments section trying to make predictions about what she will come up with this time.

Typically Riley writes fantasy, but her novellas are where she branches out. The last one she had tried was a contemporary cozy romance about a bookstore owner and a firefighter who came to put out the store after it caught fire. They rebuilt the place together and it was all soft and sweet with lots of cozy vanilla sex.

Boring.

Not the book, the vanilla sex. The book was actually really good, but I like her darker ones better. She branches into dark romance for a lot of the novellas and those ones are my favorites. The ones that tell me she has a mind just as fucked up as my own.

Riley was planning on taking some time in the sun, away from the cold New York winter. She was *trying* to go to the Maldives. She had booked a nice resort on the water that she was going to stay in, probably would have spent half her time locked up in her villa and the other half sitting in public spaces with her laptop not paying a lick of attention to anyone around her.

Where she is actually going is with me to my place in Sicily, but she won't know that until I get her there. Riley will like Italy and my place is far enough in the country that it will be easy enough to hide her until she wants to cooperate.

Gabriel had told me I am being irrational wanting to kidnap a girl I barely know. He tried to tell me that it is a very ineffective way to make someone fall in love with you, but he has been married to his high school sweet-heart for seventeen years so what the fuck does he know about courting a woman? He got the first woman who fell into his lap pregnant over a decade ago. He has no experience dating as an adult.

But I read Riley's books. I read the drafts of the darkest shit that she refuses to publish after I hacked into her computer. I know her fantasies, now I'll find out if they are more than what she bargained for. If she is all talk or if she actually has any interest in the dark side.

I met Riley over a year ago when she reached out on the dark web. Apparently some asshole was pirating her books and selling them out from under her, she wanted them dealt with. Simple enough for a hacker of my calibur.

What she didn't know was that I had put tracking software on her devices. Not because I had any special interest in her at the time, but rather because I wanted to know who I was working with. And fuck, she is amazing.

Her pen name, Maddie Luna has already published two completed trilogies which is impressive considering she is only twenty seven. She is working on a longer series now and has the first two books out. The rumor is there would be five books, but I have seen her notes, there are going to be eight.

I catch up to Riley as she's walking away from the Starbucks with her coffee. She starts to head towards where all the American Airlines flights are which *just so happens* to be the same airline I have booked our flights under. Turns out Mrs. Blakely looks surprisingly like Riley, what a coincidence.

She sits down in one of the comfy chairs before pulling out her laptop and popping in her headphones. I sit in one of the crappy ones that are all connected to each other and wait for her to get lost in her playlist which will probably only take about five minutes, knowing her.

While I wait I go to grab the "sertraline" out of my bag, slipping one of the pills in my pocket. I play mindlessly on my phone watching the time tick by, occasionally glancing up at her to check how distracted she is.

Once I am convinced she won't notice anything I move to sit in the chair directly beside her, but more importantly, the one directly beside her coffee.

See the scary thing about the bystander effect, if there are enough people around, the likelihood of someone intervening goes significantly *down*. So I don't even bother to check around me before popping the little pill into her drink. Checking around me would only alert *her*.

No one else is coming to help her.

People are inherently selfish. That's why she needs me. Riley needs someone to look out for her since she clearly can't do it herself. I intend to be that someone.

She smiles at me politely, not noticing that I just drugged her and takes a sip of her coffee before returning to her writing. Riley gets about halfway through the drink before her eyes start to haze over.

"I don't feel good." She whispers softly.

I smile. "That's okay, I'll help you, love."

Chapter Two

Riley

Everything was a blur. I vaguely remember some random man putting my laptop away for me. I vaguely remember getting on a flight. I remember bits and pieces of take off and landing but nothing when we were in the air. I almost remember being in a car before everything goes completely dark and then nothing after that.

The next thing I do remember for sure is hearing the sound of birds chittering outside a window. My head is pounding and the sunlight streaming in from off to my left is straining against my closed eyes.

I groan and try to pull the pillow my head is on over my face but when I go to move my arm there's resistance. I pull my hand again and feel something metal around my wrist. "What the fuck?"

My eyes shoot open as I realize I am *not* hungover in the Maldives which is what I am expecting. No, I have no fucking idea where I am but what I do know is that I am handcuffed to a fucking bed.

Quickly, I sit up as much as I can, crossing my legs and taking in the room around me. There is a window off to my left, I was right about that and it is open so whoever the fuck has me in here apparently isn't worried about neighbors hearing me scream.

The bed I am sitting on is made up of soft cream sheets with two pillows at the head and a comforter that I had shirked onto the floor in my haste to sit upright. The metal frame is white with a flowing shaped headboard that the other side of my handcuffs are attached to.

A dresser sits across from the bed with a TV positioned on top of it and a bathroom with no door off to the right on that wall since apparently privacy was not a luxury I will be receiving. The stone walls were painted white and the carpet below seemed to be cream as well, everything is so plain. The thing that catches my attention more than anything else though is the closed door in the corner.

I debate the merits of screaming anyways, just because whatever fucker locked me in here didn't think anyone would hear me didn't mean no one would. But if I do I will definitively at least alert my kidnapper to the fact that I am awake and that seems like a bad idea.

Fuck.

My heart races out of my chest as I try to get some kind of bearings. I start trying to move on the bed as close as I can to the window, maybe if I can see out of it I can try and figure out where I am?

Unlikely, I always sucked at geography and I could be literally anywhere.

I weave the side of the handcuffs attached to the bed around the swirling shapes of the headboard to get myself to the otherside. I do, after a few minutes of positioning myself in every odd way imaginable in what can only be described as kidnapped yoga, manage to get a glimpse out the window.

There *is* a town somewhere out in the distance but it was so far away that without my glasses, which I currently don't have, I definitely can't see it. All I can make out is faint buildings and mountains. In between those distant buildings and mountains are endless rolling hills of yellowish grass with brown and green trees dotting the landscape. All of which is no help in trying to figure out, where in the world is Riley Madison.

I'm tempted to scream, mostly just because of how fucking annoyed I am, but then I hear the door crack open. On instinct I skitter back on the bed trying to put whatever distance I can between me and whoever is about to walk through that door.

The looming man who opens it is fucking huge. I've written enough books, watched enough true crime, and seen enough news stories to know two things were a bad sign, when they move you to a second location and when they show you their face... both of which have already happened. This man not only isn't wearing a mask, he's fucking shirtless and covered in tattoos.

"Gods, I'm so fucked." I mutter out as I look over the giant in front of me.

He has to be over six feet tall, by how much I had no idea, but a decent amount. His tattoos look like they are straining against his thick muscles, wrapped around them like the ink was made for his skin, seeping onto his chest and down his abs.

His haircut looks too perfect for an asshole grunt, the black hair flowing smoothly back in a way that was beyond sexy. His green eyes shimmer with something devious as he scans me like he was looking over his next meal, which I honestly might be for all I fucking know.

Problem is, he looks like a fucking dream from one of my dark romance novellas and if I wasn't scared he might kill me I would probably jump his bones the first opportunity I get.

"Maybe if you behave." He purrs.

My eyes go wide. "The fuck is that supposed to mean?" *Riley! Don't antagonize the kidnapper.* Fucking dumbass.

He leans against the doorway, his eyes drinking me in. "Behave and find out." He promises darkly.

I gulp down a breath, my chest suddenly feeling like I had the air punched out of it. "I..." I stutter over my words. "Where am I?" Not that I think he'll tell me.

"Italy." He replies and somehow that's worse than him not answering.

"Why would you tell me that?" I question, genuinely confused.

He shrugs, "You asked." He says as if it's that fucking simple.

"Oookkaayy." I stretch out the word needing a second to get my bearings. "*Why* am I in Italy?" Which suddenly seems like the better question.

"Because I brought you here?" He chuckles as if it was a joke.

"And who the fuck are you?" I blurt out angrily before clamping my mouth shut and realizing just how stupid talking to him like that probably is.

But he just smirks. "Liam."

I reel for a second confused why the hell he is being so forthcoming. What the hell does he want from me that he's put up with my attitude and answered every single one of my questions?

Deciding that I'm no longer interested in entertaining a conversation with the asshole who kidnapped me, I start trying to move in a way that allows me to see what's on the other side of the door, but his massive frame is blocking it.

He tilts his head to the side like he's analyzing me, but there's something more animalistic than critical in his eyes as he scans me over. "What are you doing?"

"Trying to see past you." I huff.

Liam steps aside and opens the door so I can look out it. "Satisfied?" There's nothing visible but a blank wall on the other side.

"No." I grumble, settling back into the mattress.

He kicks the door closed and it slams into the frame with a loud bang that makes me cringe back. "Don't be scared, love." He purrs. "I'm not going to hurt you." He prowls closer, coming to rest his strong hands on the end of the bed. "At least, not in a way you won't like."

My heart jumps in my chest as I push myself so far into the headboard, I'll probably have the shape of it imprinted on my back later. If there is a later...

And in my fear I say the most obvious and repeated line that every girl in every TV show and every movie who's ever been kidnapped says ever...because why the fuck not? "Please let me go, I promise I won't tell anyone." But just like with all of those other girls, my pleas fall on deaf ears.

"You know I'm not going to do that." Liam answers simply.

I do know he isn't going to do that, but what the hell else do you say in a situation like this... I need to start trying to think like some of my characters. *They* have been kidnapped before. *Most* of them escaped. Just... do what they do... I think back to my character Xavia and how she got away when her nemesis kidnapped her.

Okay, maybe melting the chains with my fire magic *wasn't* an option for me in particular, but I could figure something else out.

"What do you want from me?"

"A lot of things." He just about growls.

Suddenly my crumpled up black tanktop feels all too fucking thin against his gaze. I wrap my free arm around my chest and he rolls his eyes.

"That making you feel better?" He asks.

"Yes actually." I lie, it wasn't even slightly helping with how exposed I felt in this moment.

"Mhm." He hums like he knows better.

A silence stretches between us as we have some sort of unspoken chess match with each other. After a minute I make it a game of seeing which of us can not blink longer and when he does I feel quietly triumphant even if he didn't know we were playing.

"Are you hungry?" He says, breaking the silence.

Yes, but I'm not about to tell him that. "No." I grit out, attempting to fold my arms over my chest. "And even if I was, I wouldn't eat anything you handed to me."

"Think I'd tamper with it?"

"Have you not already drugged me once?" I counter, when he doesn't respond in favor of chewing on his lip I nod. "That's what I thought."

He chuckles, but more in a way like he's trying to shake off what I just said, than like he actually thought it was funny. "If I promise *not* to drug you, will you eat then?"

"No."

"So your plan is to starve?" Liam challenges. "Because starving will help you... how?"

I glare at him. "I don't want to be drugged again." I mutter, my eyes becoming downcast because looking at him was getting too intense.

"I said I wouldn't drug you." He replies.

"And why the fuck should I believe you?" I just about shriek, hating the fact that I was showing him how worked up I was.

He was quiet for a second seeming to think that over. "You have no reason to." I blink at that, surprised by his words. "But what's the worst thing that can happen if you eat?"

"It could be poisoned and I end up dead. It could be drugged and I end up raped or somewhere fucking else. It could taste like shit and I could throw up." Admittedly that last concern is pretty low on the list right now.

"If I was going to rape or kill you I could have already." Liam answers like he's trying to reason with me? "And I promise the pasta in Italy is good no matter where you get it from."

I scoff, "Assuredly there has to be at least *one* bad pasta place somewhere in Italy." Getting distracted from the more important thing that is happening right now by his assertion that pasta is perfect here.

"Not a one." He promises.

"If I ever get out of here," I whisper. "I'm going to prove you wrong."

Chapter Three

Liam

"Gabriel." I nod as he and his wife, Gianna, climb out of his Ferrari.

I wish I could say that this trip is entirely for pleasure, but it isn't. Gabriel's family has been wanting to see him to discuss operations in New York, by which they mean they have a stupid job they need someone else to do because they don't feel like risking their own men on it.

Gabriel flew in with Gianna on his private jet, which ordinarily I would take with them, but I had to get Riley here and getting her on the jet seemed like it would be too easy. Even first class seats on a commercial plane were trash though.

"Where's my new best friend?" Gianna hums, her long brown hair blowing in the breeze rolling across the vineyard that takes up most of the land around my property. It is still the off season so no one will be working the land for longer than I will be here with Riley.

"Upstairs." I answer. Gianna starts to head inside but I wave her off. "She's not ready for company yet."

Gianna huffs. "Who the hell am I supposed to go wine tasting with this afternoon then while you boys talk shop?" Her eyebrows above her brown eyes furrow in frustration. "Gabriel made me leave Sofia back home!"

Gabriel sighs, running a tattooed hand through his short brown hair. "Gia, Sofia is sixteen. She's too young to go wine tasting with you."

"She's my daughter! I can take her wine tasting at whatever age I want!" Her Italian accent getting thicker in her frustration. "Whatever, I'm going to see... what's her name? Ridley?" And before I can have a chance to object, she's barging into my house.

Gabriel comes around to clap a hand on my shoulder in greeting. "Door to Riley's room locked?"

"Yeah." I sigh.

He waves a hand in the air dismissively. "She'll get bored looking for the key."

I huff a chuckle, that's probably true. Gianna gets distracted easily enough. She'll take one look at my wine rack in her search and probably end up camped out on my couch with a bottle of red.

Gabriel nods to the Ferrari, "Get in, we have business."

I do as instructed, he may be my oldest friend, but he's also my boss and I follow orders. I climb into his Ferrarri and feel like I'm being shoved into a too tight shirt. The car isn't small by European standards, but by American ones it might as well be a compact.

We are about an hour out from Palermo. I had told Gabriel that I could drive there myself. His place is closer to the city since he makes *a lot* better money than I do. We are here enough though on business to have it make more sense to own rather than rent every time. Plus owning places here makes it a lot easier to keep guns and other less savory things hidden instead of having to transport them over or acquire them every time.

He speeds down the country road, the sparse trees and tall grass flying by as the car carries us closer to the city. "How's Riley?"

"Mad." I answer simply.

"Yeah well I could have fucking told you that, dumbass." Gabriel laughs. "I tried to tell you that kidnapping her would be a terrible way to introduce yourself. When I met Gia..."

Then he proceeds to drone on for the next half hour about his wonderful love story with his wife like I wasn't there when it fucking happened, and making my life choices seem way more questionable than they are in the process.

"...and I never would have been so lucky had her parents not moved to the states when she started high school." Gabriel concludes.

I zone back in then, having heard this story enough times to know where it ends. "And that's great, but I don't date."

"Not since Maggie G. in the second grade?" He feigns a mock pout.

I've had girlfriends in the past, but none important enough to introduce to Gabriel. Most of them were a month or so and nothing more. I wasn't a virgin or a prude, I just never found someone who interested me, not until Riley.

"Fuck off." I mutter. "I didn't date Maggie-" I cut myself off. "That's not the point. Look, Riley is different."

Gabriel rolls his eyes. "Yeah, yeah, she writes dark romance and she sleeps on her left side and when she masturbates she makes that cute face with her mouth open."

"I definitely haven't said that last one." I grumble.

He just chuckles. "You've been watching her for months. I know you put cameras in her place cause I saw the expense on *my* cards, you're welcome by the way."

I sigh. "The Russos are the ones in Sicily?" I ask, trying to change the subject.

"Yes." Gabriel says, but he's not letting me get off that easily. "And betting on Stockholm syndrome is a terrible way to try and build the foundation of a relationship."

"I am not 'betting on Stockholm syndrome .'" I huff.

Gabriel looks genuinely confused for a second. "Am I thinking of the wrong one? Cause I know Munchausen is the one where they fake being sick right? Stockholm in the falling for your captor?"

I blow out a breath. "No, you have the terminology right-"

"Oh good." He cuts me off.

I glare at him for a second before continuing. "It's more complicated than that."

"Yeah, but it's really not." Gabriel says plainly. "You're her captor, you want her to fall for you. That's Stockholm syndrome. And if you're going to lure her into it, you probably should know that because it will make it a hell of a lot easier to give it to her the more you know about it."

"I don't like this conversation."

"I don't like that you kidnapped some random girl and brought her to Italy with you when I really needed your full attention." Gabriel counters. "We're all having to deal with things we'd rather not be dealing with right now. I wanted this to be a boys trips. Gia wanted to go wine tasting. Riley probably wanted to never know any of us. We make sacrifices because we have to."

There's a beat of silence in the car before he sighs. "Now look up Stockholm syndrome and try to learn how the fuck it works. It's gonna fucking kill you if this doesn't work out and we have to make other arrangements for Riley."

My stomach drops at the thought, but I do as he says. Knowing Gabriel the second Riley meets him or Gianna there's no turning back. Either she acclimates to us or she'll end up dead. It would be too big of a risk to try and let her go again. Hopefully Gia stays away from her until I can be more sure of if I can actually get her to be with me or not.

I climb out of the car, thankful to no longer be confined to the small seat. My gun had been tucked into the back of my waistband, covered by my black button up since we got in the car. Gabriel had said this meeting was too professional for me to wear a hoodie, jackass.

Typically he would bring someone else as his muscle, but he's traveling light this time so it's just me. We have good relations with the Russos so it would be considered rude to walk in here with a whole squadron of people all armed to the teeth. The guns we do have are to show that we were kin more than that we are actually looking to shoot anyone.

The Russo compound is huge. The orange stone walls stretch up higher than most of the surrounding buildings' fences. No less than fifteen men patrol the perimeter of the wall with at least three at the entrance and I clock them all since checking out security does fall within my job description.

The driveway is made of perfectly level white pavers rather than concrete, to show off their extravagant wealth. The same peachy stone of the walls was used to make the house, with a red terracotta roof made of curved shingles.

The front white door has six small square windows in it. The home has archways at almost every entrance and window, any that don't lead out to a small balcony. The land-scaping around their mansion is immaculate, another show of status.

Luigi Russo, the head of the Russo family, is in his mid sixties despite his wife, Mari-ana being more than ten years his junior. He comes out to greet us, his gray hair full and perfectly combed back despite his older age, he waves a hand. "Mr. Cavallo. Mr. Mitchell. A pleasure as always to have you at my home."

His son, Nico approaches from behind him, his brown eyes more watchful like he's sizing us up, he probably is and I'm sure my eyes are doing the same. His dark brown hair is styled messier, in a way more common and trendy with other people in their late twenties in Italy.

Gabriel grasps Luigi's hand firmly, giving him a strong shake and patting him on the back. "Always good to see family." He smiles like he's just here on a casual visit.

"Mr. Cavallo." Nico nods, only greeting Gabriel, knowing I'm no one of importance. I'd roll my eyes at the slight if it wasn't likely to get me killed.

"Come in." Luigi insists. "Mariana cooked dinner tonight, prepare for burnt pasta." He chuckles and turns around, wandering into the house without a second word.

Nico follows behind him like the obedient lap dog he is, although I guess I have no room to talk since I'm following Gabriel in the same damned way.

Gabriel lets Luigi and Nico lead us through more extravagant rooms than necessary to get to the dining room.

The sun had already set by the time we arrived. The dining room is lit up with three ornate chandeliers hanging from the round vaulted ceiling, all of which looked like they had fake electric candles in them. There are also a few lamps positioned around the room to give enough lighting to actually see by since the chandeliers most definitely didn't do that.

Dark wood makes up the long table and chairs, with lighter orange fabric covering their seats and backs. The table isn't covered in a table cloth, likely to show off the perfect condition of the mahogany wood.

A few house plants are dotted around the edges and the corners against the dark orange walls. There are large windows rounded at the top lined down the long side of the dining room as well as behind the head of the table. On the wall not housing the door or covered in windows is a bar that has some of the most expensive looking bottles of whiskey even *I* have ever seen and that's saying something because Gabriel loves expensive whiskey. Seems like our Italian friends know that.

"Please, sit." Luigi says as he pulls out his chair at the head of the table.

Something I didn't realize until Gabriel had to teach it to me, there's a lot of social politics on *where* at a table someone sits. Gabriel takes the seat to the left of Luigi, looking out onto the water. Nico takes the seat across from his father, to show that he is second in command. A few other random men I don't know off hand file in on the side across from Gabriel and I take the seat to Gabriel's left.

Dinner is long and drawn out with lots of drinking and casual chit chat. Mariana's food was damned perfect in spite of Luigi's joke. Truly some of the best pasta I have ever had.

After an eternity of glad handing we finally start to talk shop which is the only thing I really care about. Gabriel seemed completely in his element though, he was raised for this. This kind of long dinners and social politics had been drilled into him his whole life to the point where he didn't even sweat it.

"Yeah, some assholes who were a little too big for their own good." Luigi grumbles. "Started noticing our cars and boosted a couple of them off our street crew in Venice."

"Shame." Gabriel drawls. "Someone going to do something about that?"

"I sure hope so." Luigi nods. "But my men, they don't like to get involved once things cross the border. Monaco is a little far for my tastes."

Gabriel nods immediately, understanding the meaning. "I understand, Italy is a little far for my tastes too." He counters.

I take a sip of my whiskey, I was right too, it is fucking perfect. I simply just enjoy the smokey flavor of my drink and watch the conversation but there is no room for me to participate. This is Gabriel's business, I'm more like a bulky accessory.

Luigi smiles. "Well I'm glad you could make the trip. New York, it's such a wonderful city. I have some friends who will be in the area come summer time. You know my friends are always your friends. Right, Mr. Cavallo?"

Fuck, what ever is in these cars Luigi must want it back badly if he's willing to leave such an open ended promise on the table.

Gabriel smiles back. "You know, I do think I need to swing by Paris on my way back home. The Mrs. loves Louis Vuitton. Maybe if I see your cars, I can make sure they find their proper owners."

"That's all I ask." Luigi nods. "More whiskey?"

Chapter Four

Riley

I did eat the pasta that Liam left in the room for me but only after he left. On the off chance that it was poisoned or drugged I didn't want him to know that I had taken the bait. But the food was fine, honestly it was really good as much as I hated to admit that.

He locked the window with a fucking pad-lock before unchaining me from the bed to let me use the bathroom. He left me uncuffed after that under threat of if I tried to run he would chain me back up again and then I would have to follow his bathroom schedule. Bastard.

It is starting to get dark now and I keep hearing footsteps padding around outside my door, but no sign of anyone coming in. At the very least I did find a TV remote in one of the dresser drawers but this stupid fucking thing only gets basic cable and I don't speak Italian.

I've spent the last few hours hanging my head over the side of the bed and making up what the characters are saying with no better way to pass my time.

"Oh Paulo, how dare you cheat on me with Juan Carlos!?" I ask as the woman in the telenovela yells angrily at who I can only assume is her husband. "Oh Tina, I would never, you shouldn't believe the gardener! I–"

My words fade as the door handle to my room starts to jiggle. I jerk upright at the intrusion expecting the door to open quickly, but it doesn't.

No, instead the handle rattles for a solid two minutes before I finally hear a triumphant, "Ah ha!" From the other side as the door swings open, but it's not Liam who's standing in it.

A brunette who appears to be in her thirties and just a little bit shorter than me holds a bottle of wine and two glasses in one hand as well as what I (as an author and only because I'm an author not because of the shit I got up to in my teenage years that we aren't going to talk about) recognize to be a lock picking set. She slips the tools in her pocket, turning as she does so likely to deliberately show me the gun tucked into her perfectly white pants.

"Hello, new best friend!" She smiles, her Italian accent more understandable than any of the people on the TV.

I blink. "What?"

She reaches behind her back, her teal blouse ruffling as she does. I skitter back, terrified I'm about to get shot by this random ass woman who just barged into the room, but instead she pulls out a deck of cards.

"Ridley, has anyone ever taught you how to cheat at poker?" She asks.

"Riley." I correct.

"Riley!" She cheers. "That makes so much more sense. I was wonder what the fuck kind of name was Ridley."

I shake my head like a confused dog. "I'm sorry, who are you?"

"Gianna." She answers like I should have somehow already known that? "Or Gia. I'm sure Liam's talked about me!" When I don't respond she huffs. "Stronzo."

"I don't know what that means?"

Gia gasps. "You don't know how to curse in Italian?" She closes the door behind her and comes to sit on the corner of the bed opposite me, tossing the deck of cards down as she does. "That's simply unacceptable! If you're going to be my new best friend you have to know how to curse in my native tongue."

"I only know how to curse in english." I tell her.

"I can fix that!" Gianna says. "Okay so we'll start with stronzo. That means piece of shit. You can say it to William the next time you see him as practice." She nods like that's the best idea she's ever heard.

I shake my head. "I'm not going to antago-nize him." I respond, quickly interpreting that must be Liam's actual first name.

She grumbles. "Why not? He loves it when I do it!" Somehow I doubt that immediately. "Here, practice! Stronzo. Now you say it."

While I didn't envision my evening being spent with this random woman learning how to curse in Italian, it is admittedly a preferable alternative to making up the closed captions for a TV show I don't understand.

"Stronzo?" I try.

She shakes her head. "No, no, you have to roll the r. Like this stronzo."

I try again but fail in rolling my r.

Gia sighs. "Your english tongue can't do it."

"Sorry." I mutter, not really wanting to upset the woman with the gun.

She waves me off. "It's fine. You'll just sound like an American but I supposed that's Liam's fault for picking someone who's not Italian."

I just nod, not really knowing how to respond to anything that's happening right now. This is easily weirder than the encounter I had with Liam earlier today. At least with him everything was somewhat expected.

Asshole kidnapper trying to get in my pants without trying to be obvious. That I could handle. What I didn't know how to handle was a small bubbly Italian woman.

Gianna stands and moves over to the side table. She uncorks the wine, pouring both glasses half full before passing me one. "Drink." She tells me in a way that didn't really feel like it brokered room for discussion.

I take the glass and chug some down thinking maybe this would all be easier to handle wasted rather than sober. "Where's Liam?" I ask, settling more comfortably into the bed as the wine seems to remedy some of my stress.

"Work." She waves a hand and makes a sour face. "Gabriel and him will be back late. I was going to bring you dinner, but I didn't feel like cooking. So I bought you wine instead. That's better than dinner anyways."

I have no idea who Gabriel is but based on context I would guess Gia's husband. This is easily the most insane thing that's ever happened to me in my life. I gulp down some more of the wine trying to ignore that.

Gianna drinks some too, just about giving me a run for my money with how much I drank in one go. She comes to sit on the bed. "You never answered my question. Has anyone ever taught you how to cheat at poker?"

I shake my head. "No."

"Well that changes tonight!"

Gianna laughs loudly, tossing down her cards, "If my husband didn't already own Liam, he definitely would after tonight!" She starts gathering the cards before I really get a chance to stare at my misery.

"You said you were cheating!" I argue, draining the dregs of my wine to drown my losing hand.

She waves a hand. "That doesn't matter if you can't prove it." She taunts, starting to shuffle again. "Nothing in this life matters if you can't prove it." And when she said it, it felt like she was trying to give me some kind of advice for the future.

"I can't believe that." I say softly, reaching over to refill my wine glass on the third bottle she'd brought up. We are both pretty sloshed at this point, probably me more than her if I'm being honest.

"Believe, don't believe. You'll learn." Gia tells me, the words less ominous and more like a friend confiding in another.

She's about to deal again when someone calls from downstairs "GIA!" I don't immediately recognize the voice, so I know it's not Liam's. I'll never forget his gruff cadence as long as I live.

Gia huffs, tossing the cards down and stomping over to the door. "WHAT!?" She yells back at whoever it was.

There's footsteps coming up a staircase before I see a man with short brown hair appear in the doorway and kiss Gia. His brown eyes look over me briefly like he's assessing something. I had in fact learned that her husband is Gabriel so putting two and two together was simple enough. "Time to go." He tells her, taking her hand and pulling her from the room.

She doesn't argue, instead just waving to me and saying, "Bye, Riley! I'll see you, remember what I taught you!" Before following her husband back down the stairs.

I chuckle a little but that chuckle immediately stops when I see Liam.

He's holding a small brown paper bag of food that he brings over to me and sets on the bed. "I picked you up something."

I take the bag without hesitation this time, mostly because I'm starving after killing at least one and a half bottles of wine. Inside are two take out containers one full of calamari and the other chicken carbonara, both of which are favorites of mine. I should probably be asking how he knows that, but I don't. Something I gathered talking to Gianna was that Liam has been watching me for a while.

"Thank you." I say, pulling out the plastic wear and the container of calamari.

Liam closes the door before coming to pick up the glass of wine Gia left on the floor beside the bed. He kicks back the rest of the glass before setting it down on the side table next to the empty bottles we've finished.

"Did you have a good night?" He leans against the wall, apparently being gracious enough to give me space.

I nod, popping a piece of calamari into my mouth. "Yeah, Gia is fun." Surprising myself by that I actually mean it, in spite of my cir-cumstances.

He nods. "She's been excited to meet you."

I chew on another piece of calamari trying not to think too hard about the implications of his words, but I can't help myself. "Why am I here, Liam?"

He runs a hand through his hair, like he needs a second to try and figure out how to answer that question. "Do you remember that hacker you asked a year ago to help you with someone who was pirating your books?" He challenges my question with one of his own.

It takes me a second to remember but then I nod and realization dawns on me. "Yeah..." I say hesitantly.

"I started looking into you." He tells me, affirming my assumptions that he was said hacker. "And then... I couldn't stop." He says the words like they are an admission, like they are a secret he didn't know how to tell me. "Riley, you're amazing." He beams.

I shake my head as I continue eating. "I don't... I don't know what to say to that." There's a silence and I let myself get distracted in the food. In doing so I almost don't notice when he sits down on the opposite edge of the bed... almost.

"I know I didn't go about this the right way." Liam says and I huff in a way to say *well duh*. "But I like you, Riley. And I want to take care of you. You need someone to take care of you." He asserts.

On principle I want to object, but then I consider that he was able to kidnap me so damned easily and that he may have a point. Most days I forget to eat in favor of writing at my computer. I drink more alcohol than water the majority of the time. But that being said, if someone was going to take care of me I was more than a little hesitant to let it be the asshole who was holding me hostage.

"I don't want that person to be you." I say simply, my words slurring a little and coming out muttered.

He doesn't respond to that. Instead he takes one of the wine glasses into the bathroom and fills it with water. Liam just about shoves it into my hands, taking away my fork in the process. "Drink." He orders.

I'm tempted to throw it at him just for the fuck of it, but I know he's right and I don't want to find out what happens yet if I don't listen to him. So I take the smallest sip I can.

He growls. "All of it, Riley."

"Stronzo." I mutter as I chug down the glass as instructed, but I miss rolling the r again.

Surprisingly, he chuckles. "I see Gia taught you some things while she was here." There's another silence that stretches between us before he says, "I read your drafts."

I freeze, swallowing hard on my food as I stare down at the ground feeling self conscious as all hell and then immediately getting mad that this man could make me feel self conscious at all after what he's done to me. "All of them?" I squeak out.

"*All* of them, love." He emphasizes. "And everything you've published. Everything you've edited out thinking it was too dark for your audience..." Something dangerous but sensual hangs in the air at his words. "All the little scenes you put in a save file for when you're *alone*."

I shake my head. "I don't want to talk about this with you."

"It's good, Riley." Liam promises. "There is a reason your work reaches the audience it does. There's a reason you have the following you do and you shouldn't feel like you need to censor yourself."

"I don't want to talk about this with you." I repeat, yanking the fork out of his hand so I can go back to eating.

"You won't talk about it with your therapist. You should talk about it with someone." He says.

I reel back. "I'm sorry and you know what I talk about in my therapy sessions, how?" I balk, already knowing the answer. I wave him off. "You know what, forget I asked. Can I please just eat in peace?"

I was expecting him to say no, but he didn't. "I'll bring you up some pajamas in a little bit, please for my sake, drink another glass of water before then." And then he leaves, and somehow that's so much worse.

Chapter Five

Liam

"Gabriel, you have to give me more time." I say into the phone, trying to reason with him is like trying to tip over a bull. Which I've never tried... especially not that one summer that I was drunk off my ass with Gabriel in Spain.

"We need to take care of this shit in Monaco so we can get back home. You know I don't like leaving Dante alone for that long." He replies. "I'm not telling you to kill her, but if you can't get her to be reasonable by the time we need to leave, she'll need to get shipped back stateside so someone can keep an eye on her there."

I sigh, knowing that once he's decided something that it's the end of the discussion, but I try anyways. "Is there any chance you can give me more than five days?"

"None." Gabriel says. "You're lucky you're getting five days. Gia has decided we need to buy everything in all of Italy so I will be spending the time up to my ass in boutique bags."

"Maybe you can bring Gianna by some time, Riley really seemed like she liked her." And that stupid research I did about Stockholm syndrome talked about how much easier it is to bond with other captors when you like one of them to begin with.

There's a pause on the other end of the line followed by a sigh and then Gia chiming in. "I'll be there later tomorrow!"

"Do you see the shit you've started?" Gabriel grumbles. "Whatever, you have five days. Use it wisely." Then he ends the call.

Five days.

I can figure out how to work with five days. That's better than one or two days. Riley already likes Gia, I just need to figure out how to get her to like me. It can't possibly be that hard. There's a reason this Stockholm syndrome is so widely talked about, it's common. Inducing it on purpose has to be doable.

Most of the research I did talked about how it comes from prolonged exposure to the captor as well as having meaningful interactions and relying on them for basic needs. Some of those I've already been doing, given most of what I looked at wasn't meant to be used as a *how to guide*, but that was their mistake for having so much information on the subject.

I have insomnia, so I don't really do a lot of sleeping. Spending all night researching psychology was not my idea of a good time, but I need this to work.

I finish cooking the pancakes I'd been working on and set up my alarm system so it will go off if any of the doors or windows are opened. I intend to try and let Riley out of her room today, with supervision of course, but still better to have contingencies.

Which is why her coffee will have a mild sedative in it. Nothing that will knock her out, just something that will keep her more docile. A part of me hopes she won't even notice it, but I know that's unlikely.

I set the table with the pancakes, sausage, and bacon before pouring cream and coffee on top of the crushed up hydroxyzine in her cup.

Her laptop is on the table too, beside the chair that I have put a place setting out at for her, with the last story she was working on put into an offline Word document. I disabled the wifi and location services putting enough walls of blocks between them and her that she'll have no hope of accessing them.

Sunlight pours in through the arched windows into the dining room. My neighbor's vineyard looks like a bunch of posts but the view of the rolling hills and the mountains make it worth the few sticks in between. The dining room is painted a soft olive green color that the previous owners had picked and I just left, because I didn't really give a fuck what color any of the walls were.

I head down the hallway and upstairs to get Riley before the food is cold. Her room is the first door on the right. I turn the lock and she immediately shoots upright in the bed, panting.

"Fuck." She mutters, running a hand through her golden hair. She watches me carefully in the doorway before her eyes turn downcast like she doesn't want to look at me too long.

"It's just me." I say, knowing full well I was probably the one she was scared of. "I made you breakfast." I step to the side and gesture through the door.

Riley looks at me confused. "You're letting me out?"

"Of the room, not the house." I correct quickly. "There's alarms and locks on every door and window and the nearest people are over a mile away." I tell her, before she has a chance to get any ideas. "And don't forget I do have a gun, that I'd much rather use for that thing in chapter seventy two than to kill you with."

Chapter seventy two was a gun scene between two of her characters in one of her urban fantasy books, the male main character put his gun into the female main character's pussy and used it to get her off. I'm sure she remembers writing that.

She gasps a little, her hazel eyes going wide for a second before trying to feign composure. "I don't want that." But the way her voice quivers makes it seem like a lie.

"We'll see." I respond before turning and starting to head downstairs. "Now, let's go. Food is getting cold."

She timidly climbs out of bed and follows me down the steps. "This place is huge." She says softly, her feet padding gently on the terracotta brick floors behind me.

I pick her round glasses up off the dining table and pass them to her. "So you can actually see."

Riley smiles a little and takes them. She pushes some of her hair out of her face as she slides the glasses on. "Thank you."

I pull out her chair at the long table to the right of my seat, so she's looking out at the vineyard.

Her white t-shirt clings to her full breasts. The tight blue plaid pants hug her hips and ass going down to flare at the bottom. I had also managed to redirect her suitcase to our flight, that took a little more work.

She takes the seat and looks over the food. "You did all this for me?" Her tone is laced in suspicion which I wish I could assuage, but I am currently trying to drug her.

"Yes." I smile softly at her.

Riley shakes her head. "I don't understand." Then her attention turns to her laptop. "And you're letting me have this?" She immediately tries to open a web browser, likely to try and access some kind of chat forum to call for help.

"The wifi is off." I tell her.

She grumbles a little before closing the window. "Of course it is." She turns back to me, her gaze traveling over the food. "What do you want from me?"

"Your heart?" I shrug cheesily.

Riley scoffs. "I have a feeling that's not the piece of my anatomy you're most interested in." She counters. "What else do you want?" But this time when she says it, it's a purr, like she's trying to entice me to give an answer that's more seductive.

I consider the merits of that for a moment, debating if she's ready for me to try and make a pass at her. She really hasn't even let me touch her yet, I mean I have but she hasn't *let* me. Too soon, as much as my cock wants to try and convince me otherwise. If I said something too explicit about my intentions with her now she's going to see me as a predator. I mean I am, but I don't want her to see me like that.

"Can't a man just bring a pretty girl to Italy with no ulterior motive?" I respond, leaning in on the table to give her some semblance of closeness.

Riley rolls her eyes so hard it probably hurts. "You're so full of shit." She mutters picking up the coffee, apparently deciding her caffeine addiction and that I haven't drugged her again *yet* made it safe. "How do you say that in Italian?"

"You'll have to ask Gianna the next time you see her." No way in hell am I giving her *more* ways to curse at me, she's already called me every dirty name in the book. Not in front of me mind you, but I do have cameras in her room.

She hums into the coffee as she takes a rather long sip of it, which works out for me cause the faster she drinks it the less likely she is to notice that I tampered with it until it's too late. Then Riley proceeds to just watch me like she's trying to figure out what to do next.

"Did you want to eat?" I ask her, gesturing to the food.

She eyes me cautiously before shoving her fork into a pancake and moving it onto her plate. "This is the weirdest kidnapping ever." Riley shakes her head softly as she takes a few more pancakes and some bacon.

"Did you not want the sausage?" I ask, con-fused since it's typically one of her favorite breakfast foods.

"I don't want you to watch me eat it." She answers simply, before looking at her plate then deciding to grab a few more pieces of bacon. Riley takes another long drink of the coffee.

I hadn't been expecting that answer, but I guess that's fair enough. Not wanting to make her eat alone, I grab some food for myself. "So tell me about your parents."

Riley proceeds to sputter and spit coffee all over her shirt, before starting to cough, likely trying to get coffee out of her lungs. "What the fuck?" She grumbles. "What the hell kind of question is that?" She grabs the napkin off the table and tries to clean herself off with it as best as possible.

"It wasn't a question." I counter, making it clear telling me isn't an option, it's a demand. "You have your mom blocked under the contact 'Bitch Egg Donor' and your father is basically nonexistent. You haven't written about them in any of the journal entries you have. You don't talk about them in therapy. I only found their names by looking through your records, but you basically pretend like they don't exist. Why?"

Riley stares out at the mountains through the windows. Her fingers drum on the coffee cup, like she's looking for something to do with them. She shakes her head. "It's complicated."

"I like complicated, try me."

She glares at me for a second, clearly having hoped that was going to be enough to assuage me, it's not. Then she scoffs and takes a more controlled sip of her coffee. "Why do you care?"

"We're not talking about me."

"Maybe we should." Riley hisses. "It's your fucked up actions that landed me here. Maybe we should be analyzing your psyche instead of mine."

"You're dodging the question." I counter, not giving in to her rage, it's not meant for me anyways. She's mad at her parents and is just misplacing it because I'm the closest person to her.

Her brow creases in frustration. "If I refuse to talk about them with my therapist, what the hell makes you think I'll talk about them with you?"

I shrug. "Optimism." She chugs down the rest of your coffee. "Besides, your therapist has never given you an anti-anxiety medication before asking about it." I smirk at her before nodding at her coffee.

Riley's eyes go wide as she stares down at the dregs of her cup like she's expecting to see something in the bottom. "Fuck you." She sets the cup down on the table. "Can I just go back to my room?" She goes to get up before I answer the question but I grab her wrist and stop her.

"No." I know she wasn't really asking, but she wasn't getting out of opening up to me that easily. "Sit down." When she just glares at me I pick up my knife with my other hands and twist it between my fingers. "Now, Riley."

She doesn't hesitate then before plopping angrily back down into the chair. "I had a bad childhood." She tells me like she thinks that will be enough.

"I know that much." I let go of her wrist but don't set the knife back down. "How bad?"

Riley's lip forms a tight line. "I don't want to talk about this." She fights, but her eyes are locked on the knife spinning in my hand.

"One story and I'll let you off the hook." I promise.

She has a silent staring match with my knife before finally sighing. "When I was sixteen," She starts and I set the knife down. "My mother had a boyfriend who she kept bringing around the house."

I immediately sense where this story is going.

"I kept trying to tell her the boyfriend was bad news." Riley said softly, her eyes getting a far off look like she wasn't really here anymore, but she kept talking. "One day I got home from school and she wasn't there, she had to work late, but... he was." Riley takes a deep breath but I cut her off.

"You can stop." I tell her softly.

"No." She hisses. "You wanted to hear about my childhood, asshole. You just about fucking threaten me with a knife and now you're going to just fold?" She lets out a harsh laugh.

My stomach rolls as she continues, likely just to spite me. Some part of me is suspicious that she pulled out the worst story in her arsenal just to try and make me uncomfortable, but she's right, this is my fault for pushing. I wanted to hear about her childhood, that's what I'm getting.

"I've been drugged before." Her eyes stare daggers into me. "He slipped a roofie into a glass of tea I made after school. I had gotten about half way through my math homework before I felt his hands on me and by that point I had finished the tea."

"Stop." I tell her.

"He brought me into *my mother's* bedroom. Called me *her* name and told me I'd never looked better than I did right now." Riley said through gritted teeth.

"*Stop.*" I say stronger this time, but she doesn't.

"It fucking hurt like hell." Riley looked me dead in the eyes. "I had never been with any-one before." She goes to keep talking but I can't take anymore.

I quickly move behind her and clamp a hand over her mouth. "I said, stop." I try to sound forceful but I know my voice comes out weak.

Riley whimpers and I feel the tears starting to roll onto my hand. Her breathing becomes ragged and it's only then that I realize how badly I've fucked up by putting her back in that headspace and then grabbing her.

I'm a fucking idiot.

I let go of Riley as quickly as I grabbed her and pull her chair out, turning her to face me. I drop to my knees, rubbing some of the tears away with my thumb. "I'm sorry." I whisper.

She puts her hands on her knees and sobs softly into her palms. Her breathing starts to even out after a minute and I know the drugs are making it harder for her to truly lose it in the way she probably needs to.

Riley pushes herself upright and runs a hand through her hair trying to regain her composure. "My mother didn't believe me when I told her." She whispered. "That wasn't the only reason I cut her off... but it sure as fuck didn't help."

"I'm so sorry, Riley." I had heard countless stories like that because of what I do, but for some reason none ever hit me as hard as this one did.

She turns back to the food, more like she doesn't want to look at me anymore than like she actually has an interest in eating. "I haven't talked about it since."

I get up off the ground, my hand going to trace her jawline. She lets me before turning her gaze up to mine.

"Can I eat my breakfast now?" She asks softly, legitimately asks this time. Ordinarily I would have considered that a win because learning to be obedient will help with the whole Stockholm syndrome thing, but in that moment, all I can feel is guilt.

Chapter Six

Riley

Bastard. Fucker. Asshole. Piece of shit. Jackass. Stronzo. I'm running out of fucking curse words because I'm beyond fuming.

I hate him. I hate him. I hate him. I hate him.

I glare at Liam over the top of my laptop, thankful that he's sitting on the opposite side of the large ivory leather sectional. I can't focus even slightly on writing what was supposed to be a cozy romance novella about two highschool sweethearts reuniting later in life. The novella has instead taken a dark turn when the FMC brutally murders her high school sweetheart in a way that I can't stop imagining myself doing to Liam right about now.

Whatever, she can seduce the hot cop into hiding evidence for her instead and fuck him. It will still work, it just wasn't what I was planning. I write on whims anyways, my stories tend to change with my moods and it seems like they always end up working out somehow so it's fine.

The living room of the house opens to a patio that for good fucking measure he put a chain and a lock around the handles of just to keep me from getting outside. The room is painted a soft cream color like most of the house is with the same terracotta brick running through everywhere downstairs.

The sectional feels distinctly out of place and like it's too big for the room since it's pushed up against one of the walls. A large TV is mounted on the wall across from where Liam is sitting, but my view is of the patio I'll probably never set foot on.

I blame how lethargic I feel on the asshole who drugged me this morning. Whatever that "anti anxiety" medication was has had my head fuzzy all day, but I hate to admit that the feeling is actually kind of comfortable.

"You're not Xavia." He mutters.

I blink at him. "What?"

"You can't burn me with your eyes. Stop trying." He chuckles and in spite of myself I do too. Liam closes his laptop and looks at me with scrutinizing eyes.

"What are you doing?" I ask.

"Debating if you've had enough water to-day." He responds before setting down his lap-top and heading through the doors behind the couch into the kitchen. "Come on, love. If you behave, I'll give you chocolate too. I know you start your period this week."

All of that feels beyond invasive and I grum-ble, but I do push off the couch and follow him into the kitchen like the obedient lap dog he's trying to force me to be.

Honestly, he's right. I am about to start my period and I need the chocolate probably more than I need oxygen. I'm not going because he said so, I'm doing it for the bribe.

The kitchen is massive with huge arching windows over the sink. In the center is a kitchen island that's easily bigger than my table back home, but to be fair my table back home can seat like four people max. I don't usually have company.

Perfectly clean white marble countertops line the room with dark wooden cabinets above and below and on that counter a knife rack. The appliances are all stainless steel and clearly custom built into the kitchen.

Liam grabs a glass out of one of the cabinets near the sink and fills it before passing it over to me. "Drink."

I glare at him, but take the glass. At least since I watched him fill it I know he didn't drug it this time. I hold the glass lightly, my eyes fluttering around the room like I still can't think straight, but the effect of whatever he drugged me with was starting to wear off.

My grip loosens on the glass til it's slipping through my hands and I make sure I wait to move until I hear the glass hit the ground with a resounded CRACK. The glass splinters shooting off in every direction, but I just B line for the knife rack behind me. I manage to pull one free before I hear the gun cock behind me and my life flashes before my eyes.

"Put it down, Riley." Liam sighs.

I look over my shoulder and see exactly what I'm expecting, he's holding the gun that I definitely didn't consider he might have since apparently the drugs were doing more than I thought. His face is laced in annoyance as he watches me carefully.

"*Now, Riley.*" He growls.

I slide the knife back in the rack and put my hands in the air, assuming that's what he wants. Stupid. That was so fucking stupid.

"Go back into the living room. Sit down on the couch. If you try to leave I swear to god I will fucking shoot you." His orders are clear and his threat leaves no room for argument.

I move quickly, wanting to get away from the barrel as quickly as fucking possible. I rush into the living room and just about throw my-self onto the couch, scurrying into the corner of it trying to use it to hide in like that would somehow fucking save me from the fire that was behind Liam's eyes.

I hear an annoyed, "Fuck." come from the other room before a low growl rumbles through the house. Then there's a rustling, likely the knife rack being moved before loud footsteps pound into the livingroom and Liam is back hovering over my trembling form.

The gun is no longer in his hands as he crouches down and forces my head up from between my knees to look at him. "Now why the fuck would you do that?" His face is pinched in frustration more than anger as he glares down at me. "Here I thought we were having a nice day. And then you try and pull a knife on me?"

I shake my head trying to deny the very thing he just witnessed happen like that would somehow save me from whatever was about to happen next.

"I've been so patient with you, love." His eyes feel like they are searing my soul. "I've taken care of you. I haven't pushed for anything from you." I would correct him about that he forced me to spill my guts to him this morning if I wasn't fucking terrified as shit right now.

"And this is how you repay me?" He asks, seeming like he wants a response, like he wants a *sorry*, but I stay silent. After a moment of waiting he shakes his head. "You need to be punished."

My eyes go wide as I try to pull away from his grip on my chin. "No." I whisper. "I... I'm sorry." I mutter out, trying to dodge whatever this psycho's idea of punishment is.

Liam shakes his head. "It's too late now, love. I gave you a chance to be sorry." He looks down at me with pity. "You didn't take it."

"I..." I stutter out but he shushes me and that's somehow so much more terrifying than

anything else he could have done in that moment.

"It's okay, love." Liam promises softly. "It will be quick."

I clench my eyes closed as he grabs my chin firmly and pulls me closer towards him, but when I feel his lips brush against mine my eyes shoot back open. I gasp as he presses a soft kiss to my lips. It's not long or deep or intrusive but it's also not empty either. It was clear he wanted to do more, but he didn't. Instead he just pulled away with a satisfied smile.

My head reels replaying the kiss over and over and over again in my head. The way his lips felt against my own. The way I wanted to melt into him. The way it felt like even though it was only a brief second he was stealing my breath away. The way it felt like my world tilted on its axis.

For a second I forget he is my kidnapper. I forget he took me to a foreign country against my will. I forget that he *just* fucking pulled a gun on me because all I can think about was that mind shattering kiss.

It was so unassuming. So innocent. So not enough... I wanted more. What the fuck was wrong with me that I wanted more?

I stare at him, my heart racing in my chest as my hands against my own better judgement ball in his shirt and drag him closer to me.

Liam lets me. His breath is ragged as I pull him so his lips are hovering inches over mine. His one hand rests on the back of the couch behind me as the other comes up to brush the hair out of my face. "Riley."

The world freezes for a brief moment and I think sanity is about to come crashing back into me, but it doesn't. Instead I wait on baited breath, one full of anticipation for him to kiss me again, but he doesn't.

No. *I* kiss *him.*

I throw my arms around his neck and bring him down to me, my lips pressing desperately to his in a way far less innocent than how he just kissed me.

"Riley." He groans into me and I respond by moaning into him. Liam's lips part as our mouths start to move in tandem of each other. I feel his tongue slip between my lips in soft probing strokes, like he's trying to see what I like.

I know this is a mistake as it's happening. I know how fucking stupid I am for letting this man kiss me. I know I should push him off of me and run from the room screaming for help, but in spite of knowing all those things, I still let him kiss me. I still let myself melt into his arms as they come to hold me and pull me off the couch down to him on the floor.

I'm such an idiot, but if I know that why can't I fucking stop?

Now I don't exactly know how it happened, but next thing I know he's sitting on the ground and I've somehow swung myself around on top of him so I'm straddling his lap. I grind myself into the bulge of his jeans, now definitely having completely thrown reason and logic out the window.

Liam groans. "Fuck. Riley. No." He whispers, pulling his lips away from mine as he lifts me up and moves me off his lap. "We can't. Not yet."

I shake my head now thoroughly enraged that somehow now *he's* the one saying *no* to *me*??? How the fuck did that happen?

"Liam." I plead softly, still clearly having not come back to my senses. "Please."

He clears his throat and shakes his head. "No, Riley."

I huff, getting up off the ground and dusting the shame off before stomping over to the farthest I can get away from him on the couch and going back to writing.

Chapter Seven

Liam

I do my best not to fucking run away from her and into the bathroom, trying my damnedest to maintain the tough kidnapper cool guy persona that I've had up until this moment but now I'm no better than a teenager about to fucking cum in his pants because the hot girl looked at him in math class. Not based on true events, but if it was it definitely happened to Gabriel, not me, no matter what he says.

My pupils are dilated in the mirror to the point where the black almost completely overshadows the green. My black hair is disheveled from Riley running her hands through it.

I try to remind myself and my raging cock that I did the right thing. Leaving her wanting more was good for me. People always wanted what they couldn't have and that shit was especially true for Riley. I had seen her cry once when she got home because her favorite coffee shop was out of pumpkin spice for the season. Telling her no was the smart play even if my dick was painfully digging into my zipper right now.

I was planning to give myself another minute to calm down when I hear a frustrated shriek coming from the kitchen followed by a crash. I run from the bathroom to see Riley holding a glass high above her head like she's about to slam it down, so likely a different glass breaking was the sound I heard before.

"Is this the best way to handle your anger?" I chide her softly.

She just blinks at me. After a second she slowly pulls her shaking arm down out of the air. "What the fuck is happening to me?" She whispers more to herself than to me.

My mind immediately jumps to wanting to tell her that trauma makes normally reasonable people do funny things, but that would mean admitting that what I'm doing to her is traumatic and I really don't want her to think about that. "Put the cup down, Riley. You've broken enough of my glassware for one day. What are you gonna have left to smash tomorrow?"

Riley just kinda stares at me and my stupid joke like she's in shock.

I walk over to her slowly, not wanting to set her off. I gently wrap my hands around the cup and pull it from her grasp before turning to the sink and filling it up with water. I go to one of the cabinets and pull out a pill bottle before shaking one into my hand.

"Take this." I hand her the pill and the water.

This snaps her out of her stupor. "What is it?" She challenges apparently not to the point yet where she'll just take it and not question me.

"Hydroxyzine." I answer, when she still doesn't take it I amend. "It's the same thing you had earlier. It's just an anxiety medication with a slight sedative effect. It's commonly prescribed for panic attacks as needed. Trust me, you need it. Take it."

She shakes her head.

"I wasn't asking, Riley. Take it."

Riley grumbles before pretending to put the pill in her mouth, but I see her thumb still holding onto it and her palm it before slipping it into her pocket. Then she takes a drink of water. "Happy?"

"Cute." I reach into her pocket and pull the pill out. "Open." I tell her, wrapping an arm around her back so she can't squirm away from me.

She huffs. "Stronzo."

I chuckle. "You really like that word, huh?"

"It's fun to learn new things." Riley responds simply. "You should try it some time, heathen."

I glaze over the slight. "Open your mouth, Riley."

Her face sours before she clenches her mouth shut deliberately to defy me. "No." She says through gritted teeth.

I sigh and lean in to whisper in her ear. "Do I need to get the gun again, love?" She gasps a little. "Do I need to show you what else I can do with it besides point it at you?"

Riley shakes her head fiercely, apparently not ready to play out that specific fantasy with me just yet. My disappointed cock strains in my boxers, but I'll live.

I get tired of waiting, so I pinch her nose with the hand holding the pill. Her eyes go wide as

I see the panic rack through her, but she's a fighter so she tries to keep her mouth shut.

It's only after a solid minute and when her face starts to pink that she takes a gasping breath for air. I smirk triumphantly as I quickly pop the pill into her mouth and clamp my hand over it so she can't spit it back out.

"Swallow." I order. As she whimpers her objection I feel the pill slide against my hand, but I just shake my head. "Do it, Riley. Then we can go sit back down and you can spend the rest of the night writing and pretending like I don't exist."

She just about *hisses* at me, but after another second of our staring match she licks the pill off my hand and I hear her swallow.

"Give me your hands." I tell her.

Riley looks at me confused but does as instructed.

I grab them in one hand, taking the water from her. "Drink." I don't trust her not to have tried to hide the pill under her tongue. I press the water to her lips and slowly tilt the glass back.

The first bit spills down her chest but after a second she starts to follow my instructions and begins drinking it down. I make her drink the full glass before I set it down on the kitchen island.

"Now open your mouth." I growl, prepared to be disappointed and find the little pill hiding somewhere inside. Surprisingly she listens though and I see nothing. "Lift your tongue." She does that too and when her mouth is fully empty I smile.

I run my hand through her hair and whisper in her ear, "That's a good girl." Wanting to reward her for taking it.

She purrs a little and melts into my arm. "Don't." She mutters out. "Don't do that. It confuses my brain when you do that." Riley says, not seeming to realize that telling me that is honestly just more reason to call her that again rather than discouraging me. I want her confused about how she feels about me. It will make it easier for the lines to blur.

"But you were such a good girl, love." I hum, tightening my arms around her to support her body as it collapses into mine. "I have to encourage that." I tilt her chin up to look at me and her eyes go wide again.

Riley's mouth parts like she's expecting me to kiss her, like she's *waiting* for me to kiss her.

Fucking perfect.

I *make* her wait, I stand there patiently letting her stare into my eyes, keeping my expression soft, seductive. And when she finally tries to take matters into her own hands, when she decides to push up onto her toes and try to kiss me, I pull away. "No. Riley."

She just about stumbles back as I let go of her. Her eyes hungry and full of need as she takes me in like I'm a puzzle she can't seem to solve, can't seem to understand. Then she turns on her feet, huffs, and stomps out of the kitchen.

Riley's first book was a slow burn and she hates them, she hasn't written another one since.

The rest of the night is rather uneventful. Riley spends most of it on her laptop trying to pretend like I don't exist, until she starts to fall asleep on the couch and I finally let her go back to her room. I keep an eye on her for a while through the cameras as she gets ready for bed but when she finally lays down I turn my phone off.

There's three bedrooms upstairs including the one Riley is in and each of them have their own bathrooms. My office is attached to the master bedroom at the end of the hallway.

I'm hunched over in my office chair, my back killing me because of my posture but having no intention of changing it. I'm working on tracking down the cars for Gabriel but my attention is fully not focused on that because I'm thinking about Riley. I can't stop thinking about how her breath felt brushing against my lips when she wanted to kiss me.

My desk is a dark mahogany wood that matches the bookshelves behind me, lined with copies of Riley's work. It looks like a damned shrine to her if I'm being honest and it kind of is. I managed to get a hold of signed copies of every book she has, but those are back home in New York. I guess I could have her sign the ones behind me since she's literally two doors down the hall, but that seems kind of tacky.

The office is painted the same olive green used in the dining room down stairs. The color is featured in my bedroom too through the connecting doors as well as a few other random rooms in the house.

I push up from my leather desk chair, shutting off my computer and resigning myself to the fact that I wasn't going to get jackshit done tonight while my cock is trying to spring a hole in my pants. I move through the glass doors into the bedroom and go to close the doors to the balcony.

I tilt my head back with a sigh before walking over to the bed and collapsing down onto the olive colored comforter with the swirling tan pattern on top of it. I pull my phone out of my pocket fully intent on finding an old video of Riley masturbating in her bedroom, but when it opens to the video footage of her right now and I hear a soft moan come through the phone, I freeze.

My eyes go wide as I zoom in on her form on the bed and see the small movements of the covers on top of her as the depression between her legs intermittently changes shapes. "Riley." I groan, and almost like she hears me another moan slips from her lips and this one carries my name.

"Liam." She whispers.

I'm sure I've died and somehow a mistake has been made and I ended up in Heaven to have this beautiful woman moaning *my name* as she pleasures herself.

Riley's head kicks back into the pillow behind her as she lets another soft moan slip free from her supple lips.

It takes just about all my restraint not to run into her room, rip the covers off of her body, and replace her hand with my own. I want to show her just *why* she should be moaning my name. But I don't. I'm trying to play it slow and fucking her with my fingers is the exact opposite of playing it slow.

My eyes just watch the screen for a long moment, silently begging her or god or whoever could make it happen that she moves the fucking blanket. I want to watch. Truly watch, not just see the covers bounce. But sadly I have no such luck.

The sounds cresting against my ears are the most beautiful things I have ever heard in my life and because I don't have *that much* self control, I slip my hand down to my sweatpants and rub away some of my ache through the fabric.

I had been planning to watch Riley masturbate and take care of my own needs anyways, was this really that different from when I did it at my desk and she was at home? For some reason it felt like the answer was *yes* but I ignored that and pulled my sweatpants and boxers down anyways.

"Say my name again, love." I whisper to the screen. "Come on, please say it again." My hand starts to work up and down my shaft and some of my tension is slowly being relieved.

Riley's hips jerk up a little before she fights them back down and then grinds into her hand. "Liam." She whimpers out before shaking her head. A look crosses her face and she pulls her hands away from herself before resting them on top of the covers. She takes some heavy pants. "I shouldn't be doing this."

"No." I argue with the girl who can't hear me. "No, you should be doing this. Keep going, Riley, please."

Her head kicks back in a sigh and I can see her chewing on her lip. "I shouldn't..." Her eyes slip to the door, like she's *waiting* for me to walk in and catch her and when they do a blush crosses her face that I can see even in the darkened room.

Riley's jaw grinds as her hands hesitantly slip back down her body. "This is such a fucking mistake." She whispers to herself.

"Make it anyways." I purr to the phone. "I won't come stop you, I promise."

"I'm definitely losing it." She mutters to herself, but it's followed by a moan and that's how I know she started playing with herself again.

"That's okay love, you can lose it. You don't need it. You need *me*." I slide my hand up and down my cock, groaning in tandem with her next soft cry.

I wish I could hear her say it. I want to hear her say that she needs me. I want to hear her say it when my cock is buried between her legs. When she's at a shop and needs to use my credit card. When she's drunk and needs help getting into bed for the night. I want her to need me like she needs oxygen. *I need her like I need oxygen.* I want her to feel the same way.

Riley keeps working her body under the covers as I do the same to myself, both of us intermittently crying out each other's names at low volumes so the other doesn't hear. Too bad for her the microphone on the camera in her room is really good.

After a bit Riley's breathing starts to get more ragged and from how many times I've watched her get off I can tell she's about to finish. In response I stroke myself harder, wanting to follow her over the edge.

Riley lets out a cry that I can hear from my room even without the damn phone and I clamp my hand over my own mouth to mute the sounds of my own as I finish, shooting my cum onto my t-shirt.

When I turn my attention back to the camera Riley looks panicked, likely realizing how loud she just was and I know I can't just ignore that so I rip the shirt over my head and toss it onto the ground before putting my cock back in my pants. She's seen me shirtless before so hopefully that won't make her suspect anything.

I take a second to calm my breath, leaving my phone on the bed before heading out of my bedroom and down the hallway. I make sure my steps are steady and unhurried as I pull the key out of my pocket and unlock her door.

Riley has by this point rolled over and is pretending to be asleep. I almost want to laugh, but I don't. The covers are pulled up over her ears and I almost wonder if she's naked underneath them, a part of me wants to pull them back and check for myself.

I prowl over to the bed and as she hears my heavy footsteps approaching her she shoots upright and corrects my suspicions since she is at least wearing a shirt.

"What are you doing?" She hisses.

"I was about to ask you the same question, love." I purr, leaning against the wall beside her.

She shakes her head innocently. "I don't know what you mean." She whispers more like she's trying to convince herself than me.

I debate how far I want to push her, the merits of getting her to admit what she did over letting her keep her secret, well letting her *think* she kept her secret. Quickly, strategy goes out the window when I look into her beautiful hazel eyes and decide I want to hear her tell me what she did to herself with my name on her lips.

I nod, moving to sit down on the bed, but not touch her, at least not yet. "Yeah, you do, Riley."

I counter and she chews on her lip. "I know what I heard. I'm more than old enough to know what that sound was."

Riley scoffs and runs a hand through her golden hair, then she looks me dead in my eyes with a blank face and lies. "I didn't hear anything. Maybe your ears are just playing tricks on you."

I'm a little thrown by how easily the lie slipped from her lips, by how convincing she was like she truly meant it, but I knew better. "You can't pull that shit with me, I have cameras in here, Riley." I counter, immediately shutting the lie down. "I could just check them." I shrug, like I hadn't already watched every second of what she had done as it was happening.

She swallows. "Go ahead." She challenges.

"I'll go get my phone." I push up off the bed and only then does her bluff fold.

"Wait, no!" Riley cries, likely realizing admitting to it and having me *see* it are two different things.

I stop and turn back to her. "Yes, little liar?"

She bristles at that. "Don't check the cameras." Riley says softly. "Please, don't check the cameras."

I smirk as I sit back down on the bed and lean into her. "And why not, Riley?" My eyes bear into hers and she turns her gaze downcast, when she doesn't respond I push. "What were you doing in here that you don't want me to see, love?"

"Why does it feel like you already know the answer to that question?" She mutters more to herself than to me, but I just wait expectantly. "I was... taking care of something."

I nod, but I don't relent. I want more. "What were you taking care of Riley?"

She whimpers, but she seems to realize there's no escaping what I want her to admit. "I was masturbating." She whispers so softly I almost don't hear it.

I smile. "And what were you thinking about when you did it?"

Riley looks up then, looks into my damned soul as she breathes out, "You, Liam. I was thinking about you."

A groan slips from my lips. I see her gaze drift down and I know she's looking at the outline of my cock in my sweatpants, but I don't take my eyes off her. Riley's hand drifts a little closer to me on the bed for a split second before she pulls it back into herself, seeming to think better of trying to touch me.

Her words hang in the air between us, the tension so tight I could probably cut it with a knife. A knife I'd like to see how Riley reacted to if I ran it over her stomach. I want to see her body shiver in fear as her eyes go wide staring at me knowing I hold her in the palm of my hand.

"I know." I respond, forcing myself out of my fantasies. "Was I doing anything particularly interesting when you thought of me?"

Riley blushes. "No." She rushes out quickly. Too quickly.

"Maybe something with my gun?" I ask her.

The way her posture shifts as she pulls her gaze away from my pants makes me feel like my guess hit a little too close to the answer for her liking. "No." She says, her voice brash and steely.

A silence passes between us and I push up off the bed to leave when she stops me. "Wait." I do, turning back to look at her. "I'm... I'm sorry." Riley mutters.

"Why?" I ask, not really understanding the apology.

"Just... that I did that." She says. "And maybe even more so that you found out." Her hands play in the blankets, gripping them like she's nervous as she tries not to look at me.

"You never have to be sorry for that, love." I tell her. "You can borrow me for your fantasies anytime you want."

Chapter Eight

Riley

I spend the rest of the next day beyond mortified and doing my best not to look Liam in the eyes because everytime I do I can see him thinking about what I'm now sure he's watched on the cameras. This is a nightmare. In so many ways.

On the plus side the anxiety medication that Liam kept intermittently dosing me with was helping a lot which was starting to make me think maybe I just need to be on something in general. I don't know how he fucking knew that, but somehow that's more infuriating than that he kept forcing me to take it even when I tell him I don't want it. He hasn't given me any since this morning though so at least there's that.

The sun is starting to set out the windows in the living room, going down slowly behind the mountains in the distance as the skies start to turn to a mirage of oranges and pinks with small splashes of red and purple interlaced between. Liam has been in the kitchen for at least the last hour working on what I have no idea since we already ate dinner.

I've gotten up to seventeen thousand words in my novella and I'm pretty happy with that progress but the more I write the more I'm slowly starting to get convinced that this story is going to end up longer than I intended. Whatever, it will be the length it will be and my agent can help me figure out marketing later.

I do wonder if Anna is suspicious that she hasn't heard from me in a few days, but I do tend to go off the grid when I go on vacation so it's not that odd to assume I just would forget to message her which very much is working against me right now. Most likely no one has noticed me missing and probably won't for another month with the way I communicate with people.

I'm that kind of friend that shows up once in a weird while and it's like no time has passed even though we haven't seen each other in three months. I don't really have a best friend or anyone I'm all that close with.

Family was never super important to me. I distanced myself from the very small amount that I had when I turned eighteen, got out of high school, and was able to move as far the fuck away from my mother and her string of toxic men as physically possible. And my father? He was never in the picture to begin with and I never cared to look into him. A part of me is pretty sure my mother doesn't even know who he is even if there is a random dead man's name on my birth certificate.

A doorbell rings through the space and I look up from my laptop. I almost expect Liam to try and quickly shuffle me somewhere hidden so I don't ask whoever is at the door for help, but he doesn't. Apparently whoever it is he was expecting them.

Heels click through the hallways quickly coming towards me and I close my laptop. Gianna comes bolting into the room with a squeal. "Riley!" She cheers, coming to grab my hand and pull me up off the couch.

Her dress looks more expensive than my car. The high quality fabric is obvious just by looking at it. The tight black dress with beautiful lightly colored flowers on it hugs her body in all the right ways and her black lace heels go perfectly with it.

"Hi, Gia." I smile, surprising myself a little by how happy I am to see her.

She starts to drag me into the kitchen. "Come, we have a lot of work to do if we're going to drain Liam's wine rack."

I chuckle as I come into the kitchen, seeing two beautifully laid out charcuterie boards. One is full of cheeses and crackers paired with jam and honey in a rather pretty container. The other one is all chocolates, strawberries, brownies, and a handful of other sweet crap. There's also two glasses and several bottles of red wine.

This is what Liam has been doing for the past hour? I find myself really surprised by that but honestly, he's been making or buying me amazing food since I got here so I don't know why I'm caught off guard by this.

The chocolate is especially nice since I got my period this morning. Luckily I didn't have to face the embarrassment of having to *ask* Liam for a tampon because I snooped around and found period products stocked in every bathroom in this house that I have access to.

What kind of weird Beauty and the Beast bullshit have I been dragged into that I got taken by the hottest and most considerate kidnapper on the fucking planet? Liam is attractive in a way that I really, *really* didn't want him to be, but in my defense I think any straight woman with working genitalia would *also* be thoroughly confused in my situation.

Gia immediately picks up a wine opener and gets to work on one of the bottles as Liam and Gabriel come into the kitchen from the other-side of the house.

Gabriel takes one look at the counter and laughs. "Way to fuck up the curve, Mitchell." He grumbles, and it's only then that I realize I didn't know Liam's last name before now. "Gia is gonna think I can do shit like this for her and her friends now."

"You can." Gianna smiles. "Liam will teach you how to be a good husband. He seems to know."

"How many Prada bags did I buy you today?" Gabriel challenges.

Gianna thinks about it for a second. "Four? No, five! I forgot about the cute little one for my Beretta." She pops the cork off the wine bottle and starts pouring into the glasses.

"Okay." Gabriel nods. "Then I'm a good husband."

Gia and her wine saunters over to Gabriel, wrapping herself around his front before pressing a hungry kiss to his lips. "And I'm sure you'll be an even better husband tomorrow when we go to Dolce and Gabbana." She purrs.

He puts a hand over his heart. "Oh my poor bank account." Gabriel chuckles.

She waves him off, pulling away and saddling up to one of the barstools sitting at the kitchen island. "You'll live. Now get out so we can have girl talk." She eyes Liam. "Both of you."

"We have business we need to discuss anyways." Gabriel turns and as they leave I hear him ask Liam, "You have whiskey in your office, right?"

"Of course I do." Liam responds as I hear them disappear up the stairs.

"Come sit!" Gia smiles. "I want to hear about how far Liam's gotten with you."

I chuckle, running a hand through my hair and grabbing the wine glass thinking I'm definitely going to need the alcohol for this conversation. I lean back against the sink and sigh as I take a sip. "What do you want to know?"

Gia thinks about it for a second before plucking a chocolate covered strawberry off the sweet board and taking a bite. Once she finishes her mouthful she asks, "Have you kissed him yet?"

I chew on my lip for a second before nodding, "Yes." I grab a piece of what appears to be the darkest chocolate available and bite the corner of it. The flavor is rich and smokey making me just about moan into it.

"More than once?" She asks.

"All in one sitting, but technically yes." I tell her, not entirely sure why I'm being so forthcoming, but something about Gia makes me want to just tell her everything. "I wanted to kiss him again, but he hasn't really let me."

She snorts a laugh. "*He* hasn't let *you?*" She clarifies and I nod. "I definitely was expecting it to be the other way around."

"Yeah, so was I." I mutter into my wine glass, kicking back a little bit more of the smooth red.

"Maybe you're not being persistent enough." Gia suggests. "And that outfit isn't doing you any favors." She motions to my green cactus t-shirt that I had cut the neck out of and made into a crop top and my gray sweatpants.

"This is what he gave me." I tell her simply.

Gia shrugs. "Then you need to ask for something else because he's dressing you like a bum."

I bristle because I actually kind of like this outfit. "I would think the best option to get him to sleep with me would be to dress how he wants me to."

Gia bubbles, shaking giddily in her chair. "So you *do* want to sleep with him!" She shrieks.

My heart rate spikes and I shush her. "Not so fucking loud, he's going to hear you." But then immediately realize that what I didn't do was *deny* that I wanted to sleep with Liam.

Gianna nods. "Okay, okay." She says softly. There is a beat of silence before she speaks again. "So let's come up with a plan then."

I blink at her. "What?"

"Well he's a man. A man who's clearly obsessed with you." Gia takes another sip of her wine before picking up a cracker and places some cheese on it. "It should be easy enough to get him to have sex with you."

I chew on my lip a little bit really considering what we are talking about and sigh. "I'm not sure having sex with him is a good idea. I mean just because you *want* to do something doesn't mean you should."

Gianna thought about it for a second before waving me off. "I've never found that to be true. Anything I wanted to do, I did and my life has worked out just fine."

I want to correct her and tell her that she's clearly married to a very dangerous man, but then I consider how right they seem for each other even just in the brief moments I've seen them together. I consider that he seems to take care of her from what she's told me and that even if her life isn't what most people would typically define as stable, she seems to love it.

Maybe I could love a life like that too.

Naive and stupid to think, but Liam clearly is insane about me and honestly, it's felt good to be taken care of the last couple days. I've been able to let go of my responsibilities and let him take care of everything while I get to focus on my work.

Maybe it would be nice to have more of that.

Oh gods, I truly am losing it if I'm even considering this possibility. But for some stupid reason I find myself asking Gia, "What kind of plan did you have in mind?"

She smiles and refills her wine glass before pushing up from the barstool. Gia grabs my hand and starts to drag me down the hallway and up the stairs. "Liam!" She calls.

A few seconds later he peeks his head out from the bedroom at the end of the hall. "Yeah?"

"We need Riley's suitcase." Gia tells him.

"Second bedroom." Liam nods at the door, not bothering to question her as to why. "It's unlocked, both the suitcase and the bedroom."

"Great!" Gia smiles and then pulls me into the second bedroom before slamming the door behind us. She walks up to my suitcase on the bed like it's her own and flips it open. Gia starts immediately rifling through my clothes making different sounds to indicate how much she likes each individual piece.

I just kind of stand awkwardly off to the side, sipping my wine and waiting for her to stop looking through my shit.

"Do you have make up in here?" She asks. "Maybe I can have you do that while I try and salvage something from your wardrobe."

I set my wine glass down on the dresser before coming over to the suitcase and grabbing out my small makeup bag.

She eyes it for a second. "That's it?" She scoffs, when I bristle she waves a hand. "No, no, it's fine. You're right you have a natural beauty and you're young, you don't need that much makeup. Unlike my sister, she's an old cow."

I huff a laugh, not really sure how to react to that.

Gianna just about shoves me into the bathroom. "Go put on whatever tiny amount of makeup you actually do have."

I sigh as I head into the bathroom that is almost identical to the one in the room I've been staying in. I pull off my glasses and do as Gia says for whatever stupid reason, feeling more than a little self conscious that I'm putting on makeup for that asshole who kidnapped me.

"Ooooo this is cute!" Gia cheers from the other room. I was going to peek my head out but she comes into the bathroom instead showing me my red lace bra and panties set that I always bring with me when I go on vacation just in case I want to have a night out and try to get laid.

She hangs it over the side of the bathtub. "Whenever you're done with that, put this on."

I nod and just about poke my eye out with my mascara wand when I do, but I survive. After applying a little bit of a light brown eyeshadow and some winged eyeliner I move on to picking one of my like three lipsticks that I own, all of which I brought with for whatever reason. I go with the most subtle one since the rest of my makeup is a softer look, I think the warm pink color will match nicely.

Gia comes back into the bathroom holding up the one dress I have with me, a black A line one that opens deep into the back and dives into a V neck in the front. "This will do for now, but we need to go shopping once you're allowed out of the house."

I try not to think too much about what she just said, instead walking over to grab the red underwear off the bathtub. I look at it, playing with the lace between my fingers and very much having second thoughts. "Gia, I shouldn't be doing this."

She leans against the door and crosses her legs. "Why are you scared, Riley?"

"I'm not." I respond quickly without really thinking about it, but Gianna gives me a knowing look and just waits patiently for my real answer. After a minute I sigh. "Gia, how am I supposed to get over how I got here? How can I just forgive him and act like it's fine that he drugged me and brought me here against my will?"

She thought about it for a second, not just answering immediately, but putting real thought into her answer. "Who says you have to?"

"What?" I ask confused.

"Who says you have to forgive him?" Gia repeats. "I mean, you can fuck him and not be okay with what he did, they aren't mutually exclusive."

I chew on my lip, shifting on my feet as I consider her words. "I mean aren't I compromising my morals? Aren't I reinforcing that kidnapping me wasn't some horrible thing by giving him what he wants?"

She shrugs. "I think you're thinking about it too much." Gia said, taking a sip of my wine. "It's just sex. Sex is fun. You're attaching all sorts of other shit to it that you could just compartmentalize in favor of a little stress relief. I mean, I could feel the tension between the two of you when I walked in. Wouldn't it feel good to relieve some of that build up?"

I sigh, choosing to believe her logic instead of my own because honestly, her logic sounds way more appealing than my moral high ground bullshit. "Alright, get out so I can change."

Chapter Nine

Liam

"I was able to track down the cars to Monte Carlo." I say to Gabriel as he takes my fucking chair in my office and I just kind of hover over him using the mouse and keyboard. It's a power play, I know that and I know he's not doing it on purpose either. He was just trained to be this way, but it's still annoying as fuck. "I was able to track down who stole the cars and where they are now."

"They already sold them?" Gabriel asks.

"They were really high end sports cars they were using with already removed vin numbers. All they had to do was disable the tracking and change the plates. Luckily I know how to get that tracking back on." I click a couple things on one of my monitors and pull up the tracking data. "High end cars like this typically also have cameras which I was able to access as well. Cameras which none of these people thought to try and avoid."

I pull up a few images of the men who stole the car as well as the people who have it now. "Gabriel, meet Colette and Antoine Dubois, a rich French couple from Paris who were vacationing in Monaco and decided to buy cars from these lovely men," I point to the other pictures, "Louis Monreaux and Jean Corbin, also French, but they live in Monaco. Their usual game is stealing from the casino in Monte Carlo and its patrons. Seems someone turned them on to a bigger fish in Venice and they decided to see what they could catch."

"Yeah, well, it's gonna cost them their lives." Gabriel mutters, taking a sip of his whiskey. "What's our options for the hit?"

I smile. "Glad you ask." I pull up all the information I have on the casino in Monte Carlo. "Monreaux goes in pretending to be a high roller, Corbin has somehow managed to figure out how to rig the baccarat tournaments without anyone noticing since he works at the casino. Monreaux only plays every so often so no one has caught on to their scheme yet, but

I checked the records, not just the ones under his real name, but the ones under his fakes too. Each tournament has a prize of two hundred thousand euros, Monreaux wins about once a year."

"Not bad for small fish." Gabriel hums.

"Not at all." I agree. "But here's the fun part." I smirk and pull up the casino website. "The next tournament? It's in seven days and Monreaux hasn't won in over a year. So guess who's name is on the list to play next Saturday?"

"Louis Monreaux." Gabriel answers.

I shake my head and pull up the player list. "Adam Jacobs." I point at the name before pulling up a fake ID with Louis's picture and the name *Adam Jacobs* on it. "And even better, all casinos have to be able to offer the payouts in cash."

Gabriel smirks. "Are you telling me if we play this right, not only can we kill these fuck-ers, but we can steal two hundred thousand euros from them?"

I smiled. "I already have a plan."

"I'm sure you do." Gabriel chuckles, kicking back the lasts of his whiskey. He's about to say something else when my alarm system starts going off.

We look between each other quickly before running down the stairs. It doesn't take long to figure out what room the girls are in. My heart is pounding out of my chest thinking I might have to go on a manhunt for Riley tonight, but we make it into the living room and I see Riley is just sitting on the couch.

I let out a breath I didn't realize I was holding as Riley screams over the alarm, not realizing we are in the room yet, "Gia! You're going to get me in trouble!"

Gianna on the other hand is standing on a chair tampering with my alarm system on the doors to my patio whining, "I want to go outside!"

Gabriel sighs in relief wrapping an arm around Gia's waist and pulling her off the chair. "Gia, you could have just fucking asked instead of poorly trying to show Riley how to disable the alarm system."

Gianna angrily folds her arms over her chest, still holding a wine glass that's half full and assuredly not her first. "That would have been far less fun."

I walk over to my control panel in the corner of the room, making sure I cover it from Riley with my hand before punching in the code to turn the alarm off.

Gabriel shakes his head. "Honestly, this is my fault for not checking on you sooner." He takes the wine glass from her and kicks back the rest of it before setting the glass on the coffee table.

"Hey!" Gianna objects.

"I think that's enough for the evening." He nods towards the door. "Time to go, it's getting late. Liam, we can talk tomorrow."

I nod and move to show them out. As I'm walking them to the door I catch a glimpse of Riley out of the corner of my eye and realize what she is wearing. The black dress clings to her hips before flaring out and softly fanning around her knees picked up on the couch. I pull my attention away for a second to lock Gabriel and Gianna out.

As we get to the door Gabriel says, "Sorry about that." Which is surprising because he almost never apologizes to anyone. "Gia needs to learn to mind her manners."

I wave him off. "Don't worry about it."

He picks Gianna up, smacking her on the ass in a way that seems like a mix of annoyed and playful before tossing her into his Ferrari.

I lock the door behind them and head back into the living room, but Riley isn't there. I'm fully about to lose it thinking Riley somehow did manage to run in the commotion but then I hear more wine being poured in the kitchen followed by my name.

"Liam?" Riley calls softly.

I walk into the kitchen to see her holding two wine glasses in one hand. The deep V neck of her dress has the soft looking red lace of her bra peeking out and hugging her tits, I'm desperate to touch it, *touch her*. She looks fucking amazing, I mean she always does, but she clearly put in some effort and I can appreciate that.

I smirk at her as I lean against the door frame, my eyes drinking her in and trying to relish every single fucking bit of it. She did this for *me*. "Beautiful."

Riley blushes, brushing some of her curled hair over her shoulder. Her and Gia must have found her curling iron because her hair wasn't like that this morning. "Thanks." She says softly, before her expression turns more seductive. Riley brings me the second glass of wine with a smirk of her own.

I chuckle but take the other glass from the one she offered. She knows where at least *some* of the drugs are in this house and I'm not naive enough to put it past her. I think I'm just being a little paranoid, but then she looks surprised.

She takes both glasses and pours them out in the sink, which honestly just makes me more suspicious that she wasn't willing to drink from the other glass. "Forget the wine." Riley says, setting the glasses down on the counter.

I huff a laugh as I stalk towards her. "Did you just try to drug me, Riley?"

She shakes her head feverishly, the mood shifting immediately as she starts to back away from me. "No... I..." She stumbles over her words as her back hits the fridge and my arms go up on both sides of her caging her in.

"Yeah, you did." I growl. "Don't lie, Riley. I can tell when you lie to me." I lean into her. "So what was the plan? Knock me out and run before I woke up?"

"No." She said, her voice more honest this time.

I look at her a little confused. "What were you trying to dose me with?"

"Molly." She whispers.

My eyes go wide. "I don't have molly in the house."

"Gia gave it to me." Riley says quickly. "She thought maybe the drugs would make you more... interested." Of course Gia has molly. I don't know what the fuck she was thinking suggesting Riley try to slip me some, but that wasn't the part of what she said that I wanted to focus on.

"More interested in what, Riley?" I purr, knowing the answer. MDMA is commonly known to heighten someone's sex drive, I'm sure that's the effect she was banking on.

"Me." She whispers.

I shake my head, taking her chin softly in my hand, "What makes you think I'm not interested in you, love?"

Her hazel eyes are wide as saucers as she stares at me fumbling over her words trying to figure out what to say. She starts three different sentences all at once and I can see the way her brain is shorting out behind her eyes as she stares into mine.

"Shhh." I hush her. "Just come here." I whisper as I pull her lips closer to mine.

She tilts her head to the side as our lips lock in a kiss that both of us had been craving since our last. Our mouths move in tandem with each other in a rhythmic push and pull that feels so natural, so right.

"Liam." She moans into me and my name on her lips is my undoing.

"Fuck, I need to get this dress off of you." I lift her around the middle into my arms and she wraps her legs around me with a shriek. The heels of her feet dig into my back and her arms are around my neck as she nestles her–self into me.

Forget waiting. Forget trying to play it slow. She was so desperate for me she was willing to try and fucking drug me just to get me to fuck her. Clearly I've gotten her worked up enough if she's willing to take such drastic measures. We both need each other, denying either of us any longer would be unnecessary torture.

I carry her out of the kitchen and up the stairs, kicking open the door to my bedroom before tossing her down on the bed. Riley gasps as I climb on top of her, ripping my shirt up and over my head as I do. Her hands go to my chest as I come down to her lips pressing myself back to her again.

I want to make sure this first time isn't too rough. I know she likes getting fucked hard. I've seen how disappointed she's been in the past when the men who she brought home with her wanted to be soft. I've read her books. I know what she likes and I intend to give it to her, but I also want her to associate sex with me positively and going full throttle the first time is a sure fire way to have that *not* happen. Knife play, gun play, the mask that was in her one novella, that can all wait for a different day, because there will be more.

That being said, she still likes it rough and I fully intend to give it to her. Her thinking sex with me is boring sounds worse than her thinking sex with me is too violent. There's gotta be a middle ground somewhere in there and I intend to walk that line. This is about pleasuring her, making sure *she* enjoys herself so she'll want to do it again.

I grab her thigh and pull it upwards so her leg is bent, starting to wrap around me. Riley moans into my kiss as I grind into her.

Her hands start to travel lower on my body slipping to my jeans and starting to undo my pants.

"Riley." I growl into her as her hands start to work my jeans down my hips. My fingers dig into her thigh and she whimpers.

"Take off your pants." She whispers, more like she's begging than demanding.

I climb off of her and she sits up right as I pull my pants the rest of the way off. I grab her hips and drag her towards me. She slides closer on the bed and I pull her dress up and over her head.

My eyes take in her lingerie and I freeze for a second. The lace dips down in a V neck just like her dress. It's two pieces, the bottoms clinging high up on her hips. The beautiful red color draped over her enthralls me and I can't look away. Her soft curves and ample breasts are fucking exquisite, especially with this presentation. Yeah, that's an image that will be ingrained in my head for the rest of my life and thank god for that.

I push her back down hard enough that she bounces back a little. Riley lets out a huff of breath as the oxygen is pushed out of her lungs from how she just hit the bed. I don't wait for her to catch her breath before climbing back on top of her.

She tries to bring her hands down to touch my cock, but I decide I'm actually not quite done torturing her just yet. I grab her wrists, gathering them in one hand before pinning them above her head.

"Patience." I purr.

Riley whimpers. "Please. I want... I want to touch you."

"Do you Riley?" I challenge softly and she nods before even considering it. "You want to touch the man who kidnapped you? You want to feel my cock in your hands after I drugged you?" She swallows, her eyes going wide as she listens to my words. "You're willing to put your morals aside to let me fuck you."

Riley chews on her lip. "Liam." She whispers more like she's trying to get me to stop talking rather than moaning my name.

"I want you to really think about what you're doing right now, Riley." I tell her. "I want you to consider just *who* I am to you and *why* you're letting me do this." I grind into her, rubbing my cock over the lace of her panties. "Because if you don't know, I can tell you."

I want her to have my answer, not hers. I want her to follow the logic I lay out for her, not try to come up with some of her own. If she tries to justify this later she might come up with it being a momentary lapse in judgment, that's not what this is. She wants me, I saw what she did last night. I've seen the way she's been looking at me all day even though she's been trying not to. This wasn't a snap decision and I won't let her delude herself into believing it was to try and spare her sanity. Sanity is a fucking fools errand anyways.

"Why?" She asks softly, her breath catching as she stares up at me.

"You're letting me do this because you want me. You're letting me touch you because you know my hands will feel better than your own did last night. You're going to let me fuck you because even if you're not ready to admit it to yourself," I lean into her ear. "*You need me.*"

She nods softly.

"Say it, Riley." I tell her. "Say you need me."

Something flashes behind her eyes too fast for me to read what emotion it was before she starts to chew on her lip. "Liam." She whimpers, but it's not like she's trying to let me down, it's more like she's trying to get me to let her slide without having to admit what we both know.

"Say it, Riley." I whisper like I'm asking her to tell me a secret, one that just the two of us can share.

"I need you, Liam."

"I need you too, Riley."

I dip my fingers into her waist band, pulling her panties down and off of her body, but I leave the bra on her. It looks so damned good.

Riley starts to squirm under me, her body trying to push herself closer to my cock. A part of me wants desperately to flip her over, but I know it's better if she's looking at me so that she can't delude herself and try to separate my hands and my body from me as a person.

I run my fingers over her slit. "Fuck, you're soaked, love." I smirk at her as I pull the finger up to my lips and lick her wetness off of them. "Beg, Riley." I order softly. "Beg me to fuck you."

She whimpers as my hand moves down between the two of us to fist my cock and position it at her entrance, but I don't push in yet. "Please, fuck me." Riley's voice is full of desperation and it's only making my cock harder. "Please, I need you, Liam. Fuck me."

I slide myself between her legs and hear her moan my name as I push inside her folds. The first stroke is slow, letting her adjust to my length and size, but once I see her eyes roll into the back of her head with pleasure I pull out and slam into her hard.

Riley lets out a cry as her body jolts beneath me. Her pussy squeezes around my cock hard and I'm the one moaning then. She feels like fucking heaven.

After a second of both of us just coming to grips with what is happening I start to fuck her. I don't hold back, I don't take it slow. I hold her hands pinned above her head and *fuck* her. I thrust my hips hard and she lets out something between a shriek and moan with each one.

Her eyes start to flutter closed, her head tilting back and I want to let her enjoy it, but it's more important she's paying attention to what's happening.

I let go of the hand holding her wrists for a second and grab her chin pulling her head back up and tapping the side of her face, not quite slapping her but close. "Look at me, Riley."

She opens her eyes at my instructions and nods. "Okay." She whispers.

I shake my head. "That's not how I want you to respond to me."

Riley seems to catch what I'm looking for immediately, I can see the look behind her eyes and I *know* what she writes. She knows what I want her to say, but she just shrugs. "I don't know what you mean."

"Yeah you do, slut." I growl and she whimpers a little before letting out a moan. Her book characters have played around with degradation before so I know I'm not off base in saying that even if I haven't out right asked her. "Say 'Yes, Sir.' like the good girl you are, Riley."

"Yes, Sir." She rushes out quickly.

I groan hearing the words roll off her lips. "Fuck, yes, Riley. Good girl." I run my hand through her hair.

She goes to touch me and I debate letting her, but decide it will be more fun to watch her squirm. I grab her wrists and pin them back above her head. She whimpers more like an objection than anything else.

"You want to touch me?" I ask her.

Riley nods rapidly.

"Then get yourself free, love." I taunt her.

She huffs and it makes me smile. Fuck, she looks so pretty when she's pent up. Seeing the way her sexual energy is curling around her like a live wire with no where to go is fucking beautiful. The way her eyes *shimmer* with need for me is more intoxicating than molly.

My cock slams into her in a way that has her screaming my name and I press my lips to hers desperate to capture the sound so I can keep it forever. She moans into my lips and it feels like I'm draining the essence out of her fucking soul and taking it for my own as I fuck her. I've had sex countless times before, mostly cause who gives a fuck to keep track, but none of those times ever felt anything even close to this.

Euphoria builds between us, both of us lost in each other's bodies and I can tell she is because all she can do is pant with glazed over eyes and try to catch her breath. I intend to make that worse.

I finally let go of her wrist, actually this time and I slip my hand between the two of us, right down to her clit. As my thumb start to roll over the bundle of nerves Riley lets out the most mellifluous sound I've ever heard somewhere between a moan and a breath catch and a shriek in a way that's so fucking perfect I have to take a breath to fight the urge to just fucking cum on the spot.

She adjusts after a second her breathing not quite leveling out but at least going back to what it was instead of the ragged gasps of a moment prior. Her eyes drift down between our bodies as she chews on her lip like she's trying to fight the urge to scream in pleasure.

I keep working her, feeling her clit swell and her pussy clench around me as she gets closer. "Cum for me, love." I demand softly. "I want to feel you finish on my cock."

Riley nods feverishly as she rolls her hips into my body and I feel myself right on the edge too. As if we're one we both go tumbling over, her cunt gripping my dick gloriously as she pulses and I shoot ropes of cum inside of her greedy pussy.

I give us both a second to catch our breath and recover before I pull out of her. I lay down on the bed and pull her into my chest, wanting her to hear my heartbeat racing because of her, not for any sort of sinister reason, just because of something primal in me wanting her to know how worked up she gets me.

Riley and I are quiet for a while, both of us riding out our post orgasm high as we recover from what just happened between us but when the silence is finally broken it's by Riley. She jerks upright suddenly. "Liam, you have my birth control." She says with wide eyes like she's surprised she didn't consider that possibility until now.

I however did consider that before now and decided that I was willing to take the risk. I just nod. "Yeah." I confirm as if to say, *so?*

"I need that." She insists softly.

I pull her back down to me on the bed and shrug. "Do you really though, love?"

Riley turns her head up to stare at me. "Liam, I'm fucking serious, I want my birth control back."

"Fine, I'll slip it in your coffee tomorrow morning." I chuckle, brushing some of the hair out of her face.

She bristles. "No, I want to *know* I'm taking it. I don't trust you not to just *claim* you slipped it into my coffee." She already knows me too well because when I *did* want to start trying, which isn't actually right now, I absolutely would just stop slipping it to her and not say anything.

I sigh. "Fine, I'll look for it in your suitcase." I tell her to lightly confirm her suspicions about that I had no intention of giving it to her, even if that isn't true I want her to think it is.

"Thank you." She says, before tacking onto the end, "Sir."

I groan. "Don't do that, you'll start something I don't know if I can finish right now." That fucking took a lot out of me.

"Do what, Sir?" Riley purrs, tossing a leg over me and starting to grind into my chest.

My cock stirs and I know I'm already exhausted but the rest of my body is gonna have to just figure it the fuck out because I'm not fucking stopping until Riley is passed out and can't fucking walk tomorrow.

Chapter Ten

Riley

I am so fucking sore. Liam let me sleep in his bed, seeming to trust that I had no intention of running. That or maybe he locked the door when I wasn't looking. I have no idea and probably never will because he got out of bed long before I did and I passed out at some point in between him eating me out and the third time we fucked with no recollection of when.

Last night was amazing. I have never had sex feel like that before. The high was unexplainable. It was like something in my body just responded to his, like I was made for him and he was made for me. It was like he knew every single damned thing I like and then played me like a violin. Even if he did know everything I like, that only gets him so far, he also has incredible rhythm and his touch between my legs is euphoric.

Not to mention, and I know this isn't important but, his cock is fucking huge. And while that's not the *only* thing that matters it sure is a nice bonus when the man you want to fuck is hung like a horse.

I sit upright, groaning a little in pain as I do either from how many times he spanked me the second time we fucked or from how hard he went I don't know. Everything fucking hurts but in the best way. I stare out the glass balcony doors at the rising sun coming up over the mountains in the distance. The view is fucking breathtaking and it feels more like waking up in bed with someone I care about instead of with my kidnapper.

This man has me all sorts of fucked up.

He must have known I was awake because a few minutes later, Liam comes through the door holding a cup of coffee and my birth control pills, thank the gods for that. I do not want to get pregnant. I wanted to fuck him, still kind of do, but having his kids is an entirely different thing.

Liam hands me the cup of coffee and I take it with a smile. I sip and moan at the warm buttery taste, no idea what he put in it, but it's amazing. Speaking of what he put in it.

"Are you drugging me today?" I ask, taking the birth control out of his other hand and throwing back today's dose before setting it down on his night stand.

He shrugs. "Guess you'll just have to finish your coffee and find out, won't you?"

I glare at him a little but drink the coffee anyways. At this point, who fucking cares? Besides the coffee tastes really fucking good. Say what you want about the man, but he would kill as a barista. Maybe he should consider that if the whole mob thing doesn't pan out. Which I have inferred by this point is what he does. He didn't explicitly say as much, but it wasn't a stretch to figure out. He didn't exactly hide it from me.

Liam sits down on the bed beside me. He kisses my forehead and murmurs into my temple, "Such a good girl."

I mewl a little and lean into him, not really being able to help myself. I'm definitely starting to question my sanity especially with how fast this all happened, but at the same time, I'm not sure I care. This man is clearly crazy about me, is how we met really all that important?

I like him. He likes me. Shouldn't that be what mattered? Maybe I can overlook how he got me here. I sound insane. I know I do, but I've never seen someone this interested in me before. I've met someone able to work my body like he can. I'm not saying I forgive him, I definitely don't and might never, but maybe I can come to terms with this.

"I feel like I'm losing my mind." I huff into my coffee. I take a sip, letting the beverage warm me and pull me away from my thoughts. But of course Liam wants to unpack that.

"What makes you say that, love?" He asks, brushing some of the hair away from my eyes. He pulls my glasses off the bedside table and hands them to me.

I put them on with a sigh. "I just... Why am I becoming okay with this?" I huff a chuckle even though it doesn't feel funny. "I don't understand why I'm letting myself... like you?"

"Cause I'm hot." He says vainly and when I roll my eyes he chuckles. "Riley, I've put in a lot of effort to make you comfortable, despite how I got you here and have been doing everything imaginable to get you to like me. Honestly it would be more concerning for your sanity if you felt nothing for me."

I chew on my lip as I watch him, considering his words. "So it's an act?" I ask, scared that once I fall the sweet side of him will disappear.

He shakes his head. "No, love." He promises softly. "This is me."

"If this is you," I smile a little, "Then I think I like you."

Liam leans in and kisses me, he tastes like smoke and I'm a little surprised by that because I haven't seen him smoke up until this point.

"Cigarettes?" I ask.

He shrugs. "Nasty habit." When I level a rather judgmental look at him he huffs and lightly says, "Riley, I've been stalking you for almost a year and I went through your suitcase."

"So?" I scoff.

"I saw your vape." Liam says.

I grimace. "Nasty habit?" I shrug the same way he did.

Liam chuckles. "Mhm."

I chew on my lip again, debating before saying, "Can I have it?"

"Were you not just judging me less than a minute ago for the fact that I was smoking this morning." Liam counters.

"Maybe." I look down into my coffee and repeat my question. "Can I have it?"

He sighs, but walks out of the room. Liam comes back a minute or so later and tosses the vape at me. I catch it as he says. "Those things will kill you, you know."

I roll my eyes. "Yeah and cigarettes won't?"

"Is this our first fight?" He purrs.

"No." I balk a little. "I just think you shouldn't smoke." I tell him, before hitting my vape like a total fucking hypocrite.

"Ditto." Liam says leaning against the wall.

"This isn't smoking." I counter.

Liam gives me a knowing look. "You're right, it's vaping which is arguably worse, Riley." He says. "Do you know how many studies have been done about how bad vaping is for you?"

"Probably not as many as there have been for how bad cigarettes are." I mutter.

Liam turns and starts to walk out of the room. "Come get breakfast." He says, heading down the stairs without waiting for me.

"I don't have clothes!" I shout after him.

"Then be naked!" He shouts back.

I take another hit of my cherry vape before setting it down on the nightstand and getting out of bed. I search for my dress from last night, looking for something to cover myself with, but don't find it. My suspicion is that the fucker hid it considering I was reasonbly confident that it had just ended up flung onto the floor.

By the time I finish my coffee, not feeling anything beyond the caffeine buzz, I decide to give up on my search and instead try to get to my suitcase. I leave the coffee cup on the dresser before heading to the other bedroom and trying to open the door. It's fucking locked.

I huff and grumble a little. I go back into the bedroom and start rifling through the dresser drawers. I pull one open and see a bunch of t-shirts. I briefly consider that I'm probably encouraging him if I walk down there in one of his shirts, but at the same time it's kind of cold in the house and walking down there naked with my nipples in stiff peaks isn't much better.

I pick out a gray shirt and pull it over my head. It's definitely too big on me, flowing over my body gently and covering just the tops of my legs, but it's definitely better than nothing. I go to the attached bathroom and am very happy to find tampons so at least I won't bleed all over the dining room furniture.

The smell of bacon comes rolling up the stairs as I leave the bedroom and my stomach growls at me, begging me to go eat some. The salty smoky flavor sounds amazing right about now.

I pad into the dining room on soft feet and find Liam drinking his coffee. His eyes lift up from his laptop to me and he closes it when I come in the room. He smirks as he takes in me wearing his t-shirt. "I see you found clothing. I'll have to do a better job hiding it next time." But the devilish look in his eyes makes me think he doesn't actually mind that much.

I roll my eyes and come to sit down next to him at the table. He made crepes this morning with glazed berries and of course bacon and sausage. I ogle the food for a second before starting to put a crepe together with berries and bacon inside. The fact that he's a good cook on top of everything else? Yeah. He's right. I never stood a chance.

"Why?" Liam asks with a chuckle as I crush a piece of bacon into my crepe.

"Salty sweet." I supply simply before rolling the crepe and starting to cut it with the butter knife that he did allow me to have. I take a bite and moan around the combination in my mouth.

He just laughs. "Whatever you want, love."

"Whatever I want?" I ask, curiously, wanting to see just how much he means it.

Liam eyes me skeptically. "Maybe." He corrects. "Depends what you're about to ask for."

I think about it getting lost in my food as I try to figure out what the best thing to ask for is.

Do I still want to leave? Do I still want to try and call for help? I could ask for something to do that. Or do I want to see where this goes? Do I want to make sure no one comes to interrupt the little bubble he's created for us?

After a minute of me not answering Liam turns back to his laptop and starts working on something, but I have no idea what. He might be the only person I know though who types faster than I do. His fingers fly over the keyboard at a rate that has to be closer to ninety to one hundred words per minute. I average seventy to eighty so he's far out doing me.

I watch the birds soar over the empty vineyard out the window, trying to grapple with what the fuck I'm supposed to do now. "Where is this going?" I ask him.

Liam finishes up what he's typing before closing the laptop again. "What do you mean?"

"I mean, what is this?" I ask. "Like what do you want this to be? Do you intend to just hold me forever? Do you want something real?"

Liam chuckles. "Are you trying to have the relationship talk with me?"

"I guess." I shrug. "But I'm also a hostage asking her kidnapper if I'm ever going to be free again." I say a little more sadly.

He looks me over for a second, seeming to consider his words before answering. "From me? No. You'll never be free of me again." My stomach drops a little but he keeps talking. "But if you're asking if I intend to keep you locked away from society." He sighs a little.

"As much as I selfishly might want to, that wouldn't be fair or healthy for you and I only want what's best for you, Riley."

I let out a little bit of a sigh, feeling slightly relieved. "So... what happens now?"

"We go to Monte Carlo." He answers and I get really fucking confused. "I have some business in Monaco at the end of the week and then Paris. You're coming with me, so long as you can behave."

I nod. I don't exactly know what his definition of *behave* is, but I'm sure I can figure out how to comply with it. "Okay." Besides, I've never been to Paris and writing in a Parisian cafe sounds like it would be super fun if I can figure out how to get him to let me do that.

"As for what this is." Liam says. "I intend to put a ring on your finger by the end of the month and use it to handcuff you to my side forever." My eyes go wide with how forward he is. "I took you because I saw you and I knew you were *mine*." And as he says it I'm almost sure he's quoting one of my books on purpose.

"So that makes you my boyfriend right now?" I ask with a chuckle, trying not to show how much him saying those words to me seared through my soul.

Liam shrugged. "You can call me whatever helps you sleep easiest at night right now. But by July, you'll be calling me husband." I just about choke on my food. "You wanted a June wedding, right?"

I pull the napkin over my mouth coughing through my words. "You have to be joking."

"Do I look like I'm joking?" He asks simply.

"You're insane." I chuckle, trying to process what the fuck he just said to me. He intends to marry me? In five months??? No fucking way.

"We've established that." Liam says. "But even if I have to be holding the shotgun myself, Riley. You're walking down that aisle." He casually takes a sip of his coffee. "Paris has some really nice wedding dresses. You can go with Gianna when we're there."

I just stare at him because what else am I supposed to do when he says something like that. While I am sure I'm having heart palpitations, at least I do know he's planning to let me go out in public. "What the fuck?" I mutter, my eyes fluttering as I attempt to process what he just dumped on me.

"Don't worry, I'll give you my black card." Liam tells me, like *that* was my concern with all this. "I'm sure whatever boutique Gianna picks will be expensive so I'll take care of it." And while I do appreciate that, I think? I still look at him like he's lost his mind. He has, hasn't he? I'm the sane one, right? Everything feels so upside down I'm not actually entirely sure.

"More coffee, love?" He asks, getting up and kissing me on the cheek in a way that feels so normal despite everything that's happening around us. Liam walks into the kitchen leaving me to pick up the pieces of this conversation *on my own.*

"What the actual fuck?"

Chapter Eleven

Liam

Riley and I proceed to spend our remaining days in Italy either working or fucking. She hasn't asked any more questions about us getting married, it seems like she's just trying to ignore that fact, but I fucking mean it. I'm not going to make her change her pen name, but her legal name? That's fucking mine. She'll be Mrs. Riley Mitchell by the end of the year.

She's gotten up to twenty six thousand words in her novella and keeps complaining about how she would be further along if I didn't keep distracting her. I told her she could go back upstairs to her room if she wanted some peace and quiet. For some reason she didn't seem to like that idea and then she showed me how distracted I was making her by wrapping her lips around my cock. In her defense I had challenged her earlier to see how many words she could write in a half hour with my tongue between her legs (the answer was about fifty) so turnabout is fair play and all that.

I'm looking through everything I can find on Monreaux, Corbin, and the Dubois couple. Gabriel and I have a pretty solid plan worked out for how we're going to kill the thieves and get the cars back. If we don't have to make the Duboises casualties we won't, but the cars are coming back one way or another, it's their choice if they want to stand in the way of that.

Riley is starting to yawn more frequently next to me. I've thoroughly stopped paying attention to what I was doing at this point in favor of playing with her hair and reading over her shoulder as she types. She's cuddled into me on the couch in the living room and has been since she pulled her lips off my cock an hour or two ago.

She's gotten a lot more comfortable with me since the first time we fucked. Her viewing me as a captor seems to be easing off. I don't exactly know how she looks at me now, but the hostility of the first couple days is long gone. I was even able to let her sit out on the patio at one point for a little while, with supervision of course.

I did it as a test. I wanted to see if she was getting to the point where I could bring her out in public without having to worry too much about her running or trying to get help. I even walked into the kitchen at one point leaving her alone. I half suspected Riley to be gone by the time I got back with more coffee, but she wasn't. Honestly she seemed too invested in what she was working on to have even noticed I had walked away.

Riley went back to the guest bed for one of the nights, seeming like she needed some space to put her head back together, so I let her, but most of the time she's been in ours. I made sure to move all my guns to my safe or a different locked room and I've still been locking the door to the bedroom when we went to sleep, but she hasn't tried to leave. That fact makes me infinitely happy.

Another yawn slips past her lips and I see her eyes drifting open and shut, pausing in the middle of sentences as she just about passes out on the couch.

I shake her a little. "Riley." I whisper, taking the laptop from her. I save her work before closing it and stacking her laptop on mine. "Riley." I repeat softly.

"Hmm?" She mutters, her hands trying to go to the keyboard that's no longer there.

"Time for bed." I tell her, getting up off the couch and helping her to her feet.

Riley runs a hand through her hair as she stands with closed eyes. She's clearly burnt herself down to the wick, but I should have expected that. When I was stalking her there were many nights she fell asleep at her desk.

I pull her softly up the stairs and to our bedroom, guiding her over to the bed before heading into my office to plug in the laptops. When I turn around I expect Riley to be passed out, but instead she's at the door to my office looking in.

Her eyes scan the walls and land on the two rows of shelves I have dedicated to her. She makes herself at home, coming inside to look at my books. Riley however doesn't immediately go to hers in favor of browsing the rest of my shelves. She picks up a few books, not really saying anything before setting them back down.

Most of my shelves are romantasy (since that's Riley's genre I've looked into other similar works), dark romance, and general fantasy, but I have a decent amount of the classics interlaced between them too.

Riley pulls *The Priory of the Orange Tree* off the shelves and runs her thumb over it, riffling the pages. "This book is fucking huge, but it's so good." She runs her thumb over the blue dragon on the cover. "I wish I could write something this good."

"You have." I tell her.

Riley shakes her head. "My writing style will never be like that." She sets the book back on the shelf like she doesn't want to look at it anymore. "I know I can write a book of that size and I have, but writing a book in that *tone?* I can't do that."

"You're your own author, Riley." I walk over to her and run a hand through her hair when I do she looks up at me. "You're never going to write like Samantha Shannon because you're *not* Samantha Shannon. And that's okay. Because no one else is ever going to write like Maddie Luna because they aren't *you*. And for what it's worth. I really like Maddie Luna's writing."

She smiles and chuckles a little. "I can see that." She nods to my shelves of her books. I have at least two of each book she's published and that's just here.

Riley moves over to my small shrine and runs her fingers over the spines of her paperbacks. "Signed copies?" She asks, pulling one off the shelf to check.

I shake my head. "Not these ones. Back home, yes, but I was only able to get so many."

Riley nods, playing with the pages a little before she sheepishly asks, "Do you want them to be signed copies?"

I nod, trying not to show that I'm actually really fucking excited to have her sign my books. It kinda makes me feel like a stalker fan which I guess I am if you think about it too much, so... don't think about it?

"Yes, please, love." I grab the nicest pen I have off my desk before passing it to her.

She chuckles a little. "You know that's what Creed calls Xavia." Her hand flies over the inside cover signing the first copy before looking up at me like she's thinking.

"Why do you think that's what I call you?"

Riley blinks for a second. "Seriously?"

"Did you think I came up with that on my own?" I move to pull out the desk chair for her so she can sit down while she signs them. It's roughly thirty books, this is going to take a while.

She shrugs, "I just hadn't really thought about it." She starts to write something in the book. I try to peek over her shoulder to see what it is but she waves me off. "You can see when I'm done."

I sigh, but just start pulling the books off the shelves, stacking them next to her so she can just sign them quickly.

"Usually when I do this I'm just signing pages that get stuck in later." She doesn't write in the rest of them, just the first, but she then proceeds to bury it under the rest of the books. "That or I'm at a convention or something and I don't really get time to actually talk to the readers." She quickly signs a book and moves it over to the finished stack. "This is... different."

"You're telling me most of your readers don't kidnap you first before asking you to sign their books?" I ask with the straightest face I can muster.

She laughs. "Only the hot ones who work for the mob."

"It's not the mob." I correct softly.

"It's the mob." Riley insists. "It's fine, I don't really care what you do. You have a house in Italy, fuck like a god, and make me coffee every morning. For all I care you can be a Russian spy, I'm here for the perks."

I say the one Russian phrase I know in a very thick accent. It roughly translates to "Give me the pizza or I'll cut off your thumbs." But the sound of it is enough to make Riley jolt and look upwards in shock. I laugh, hard before telling her, "I'm fucking with you."

She sighs a little. "You're a jackass."

"You're stuck with me regardless." I tell her and she rolls her eyes. She signs a few more books before I say, "Is it tacky of me to ask you to sign the rest of them when we get back home?"

But she doesn't answer that question, instead focusing on the last words. "*We* get back *home?*" Riley clarified and I nod. "Like... living together?" She chews on her lip as I nod again. "Did you *ask* me to move in with you?"

"Did I ask you to come to Italy with me?" I reply simply.

Riley just stares at me. "Oh my gods you're serious about this." She keeps signing. "Liam-" She starts to object but I cut it off not really wanting to repeat the marriage conversation.

"I already had someone move all of your stuff to my penthouse in Manhattan." I tell her and her eyes go wide.

"You can't just do that!" She huffs, her signature angrier on that book.

"I did, Riley." I respond as if it's that easy, but I know it won't be. "Your stuff is currently sitting in boxes in my living room." Her mouth is gaped open but I keep pushing. "We'll put away what fits when we get back and we can put the rest in storage if you don't want to give it away."

"I have my own life there, Liam!" Riley rages. "I have my own place with my own shit in my own name!" She was going to keep going but I stop her again.

"*Had.*" I correct her. "You *had* those things." She swallows. "But your life is not your own anymore, Riley. It's mine." I spin the chair and put my arms on either side of her. She looks up at me with wide defiant eyes but I shut it down. "And if you had that much of a problem with that, why didn't you try to run when I left you alone outside?"

Riley growls. "Fuck you."

"We could fuck right now, Riley, but I think that would just make you more confused." I purr, my hand coming up to her face and running down her jawline.

She looks down at the pen in her hand, fury clouding her vision.

I cut off the train of thought. "If you stab me with the pen, I'm going to have to start drugging you again since you'll have proven you can't be docile."

Her eyes shoot up to me and the pen drops from her fingers. "You're a fucking monster." She sneers and it feels like she's just fucking trying to hurt me, but that doesn't mean it's not working.

I know I'm a cruel bastard, I've been told it countless times in my life before, but I don't like hearing words like that come from Riley. I've done everything I can to take care of her. I want her to see me as a protector, not as an aggressor.

I try to rationalize, both with myself and her. "You're raging out because you're grieving the life you lost by starting to accept the life I'm giving you."

"I'm raging because you're a sociopath who locked me in a house in Italy with no communication with the outside world and no option to leave!" She hisses.

"You could have left earlier today." I counter, trying to drill into her that she did at least on some level make a choice to stay. "Why didn't you?"

"Lapse in judgement." Riley grits out.

"You said you like me." I push. "I didn't make you say that, Riley. You said that. You've not asked to leave once in the past three days. And when I gave you an out, *you fucking stayed.*" Her eyes bear into me as she listens to my words. "I know you're scared of how fast this is moving. I know the way we met is questionable at best and would put me in jail for the rest of my life at worst. And I know you think I'm being crazy. But I care about you, Riley. I want to take care of you." Her face softens a little at that. "And I can't do that if you're halfway across the city."

"I'm not going to tell you that I'm okay with this." Riley answers bluntly.

"I wouldn't expect you to." I shrug. "I just want to know you're not going to get yourself hurt trying to fight me on it."

She bristles and pushes the chair away from me. "I need to finish signing these."

Chapter Twelve

Riley

"Take this." Liam orders, giving me the little pill I've come to recognize as hydroxyzine and a coffee in a to-go cup.

"Are you fucking serious?" I hiss, but I kick back the pill with no arguments and take a long sip of the coffee.

"Open." He tells me. "Tongue up." He checks my mouth, grabbing my chin softly. "Let me see your hands." He takes the coffee back from me.

I grumble but hold my hands up, fingers spread wide. "I took it." I huff, more than a little annoyed that he doesn't trust me right now.

"After that fight last night, I have to be sure." Liam hands me back the coffee. "I have to take you out in public today and I would have felt a whole hell of a lot better about that had you not decided to pick an argument with me last night."

I grit my teeth and fight the urge to tell him that he fucking started it. Instead I just take a sip of my coffee. "Can I have my phone back yet?"

"Why do you want it?" He asks.

I didn't have a good answer for that. I could make up some bullshit about how it would be easier to write on the plane with or how I need to reach out to my agent or make sure my friends haven't noticed me gone, but he wouldn't listen to any of that. "Nevermind." I huff.

It wasn't that I was going to try and call for help. But I did intend to message my therapist and ask her if I was losing it for considering this and I had a feeling Liam would be less than thrilled by that. My therapist could in theory call for help on my behalf if she felt like I was in enough current danger without violat-ing her legal requirement for confidentiality. And honestly that was a real possibility.

Liam looks at me a little suspiciously before deciding to just move on. "Did you remember

to grab tampons when you packed your suitcase?"

"Yes." I grit out, rather annoyed that we are
talking about this.

He nods before reaching into his pocket and
bending down on one knee. I just about have
a heart attack but then he lifts up my foot and
places it on his knee. Liam clips a metal ring
around my ankle before setting my leg back
down and moving back to his feet.

"What is that?" I ask.

"A tracker." He answers.

My eyes go wide. "Fucking–" I mutter annoyed, but he cuts me off.

"Did you think I would just trust you to
galavant around Europe without me having
some kind of way to find you?" He asks softly,
moving in to wrap an arm around my back
in a way that's seductive and confusing my
annoyed brain. Liam starts pressing kisses to
my ear and my jawline. "I have to keep track of
what's mine, Riley." He purrs, tilting my chin
up to him and pressing a kiss to my lips.

Suddenly I'm no longer so offended by the
clunky piece of metal attached to me. I lean
into his kiss and feel his tongue slip quickly into my mouth before pulling away. Dis-

appointment floods me as the warmth of his body leaves mine.

"It won't come back off without a key, and don't for a second think it's the only tracker I have on you." Liam tells me quickly, like he's trying to stop me from getting any ideas. "There's no escaping me, love." He promises softly before smacking me on the ass hard.

I gasp a little before grounding myself in the taste of my coffee. Slowly I start to feel the calming effect of the meds he gave me and begin to relax. This is going to be an interesting day for sure.

Liam packs our luggage into his Fiat, which I'm very surprised is the car he has here, before locking up the house and getting me into the car. "We'll meet Gabriel and Gia at the airport."

"How can I go through airport security with this thing around my ankle?" I challenge, leaning back into the seat as he pulls out onto the small road that leads away from the house.

"You won't have to, we're flying private." He answers simply. "Gabriel has a plane which is usually how I fly most places, but I had to make different arrangements when I grabbed you." He smirks a little like he's proud of that.

I roll my eyes. "Yeah, well any dumbass can kidnap a woman in an airport."

"Really?" He asks incredulously.

I take a sip of my coffee before muttering into it, "No." He laughs a little. "Honestly I'm really surprised you didn't get caught doing that."

"People in that big of public settings don't pay nearly as much attention as they think they do." Liam answers simply. "They watch for things happening *to them,* they don't watch out for other people."

"Lovely." I grumble.

"People are inherently selfish creatures, Ri–ley." Liam says. "Life is a lot easier when you accept that and look out for yourself."

"That's so cynical!" I sigh. "Don't you think there are at least *some* good people out there. *Some* who aren't selfish."

He thinks about it for a second, like he doesn't want to just dismiss me on principle, but he does still dismiss me anyways. "No, but I'm not saying that's a bad thing. If you don't look out for yourself, who will?"

"You look out for me." I counter. I may not like the way he's done so up until this point, but I can still say with absolute certainty that Liam *does* look out for me.

"Yes, because I want to read the rest of *The Deserted Violet Mountains* series and feel my cock between your legs again. Both of which are selfish reasons that I'm keeping an eye on you." Liam watches the road as we drive past the rolling hills I've been seeing out the window for the past few days.

I scoff. "So you're holding me hostage for my books and my pussy?"

Liam smirks at me. "Is that a bad thing?"

I chew on my lip considering it for a moment. "I want to say yes, but honestly no."

The rest of the ride to the airport is filled with softer conversation topics. A lot of which are Liam picking my brain about *The Deserted Violet Mountains*. I've never had a boyfriend? (I'm gonna go with boyfriend) who was this interest in my writing. It's kinda nice to be able to talk about my work with someone who cares about it.

The airport is about an hour away in which time I finish my coffee and get very sad that I won't be able to get Starbucks after going through airport security like I usually do. Liam pulls into a private parking lot that he needed a code to get into and parks in a numbered spot next to a Ferrari that I can see Gabriel and Gia making out in the front seat of.

I chuckle a little as Liam helps me out of the car and then knocks on their car window. Gabriel and Gia both flip him off before fixing their clothing and climbing out of the car.

"Stronzo." Gia mutters, pulling her elegant yellow dress down a little. She then proceeds to come around and hug me before pulling back and tsking. "Riley, why are you dressed like a peasant? Hasn't Liam given you his black card yet to fix your wardrobe?"

I bristle a little, rather liking my black skirt and pink crop top. "I don't look that bad." And next to Liam with his hoodie and jeans that's true, but then I look at Gabriel with his button up and slacks, not to mention Gia, and feel very underdressed.

"Gabriel, amore, we can go shopping in Monte Carlo, right?" Gia purrs, running one hand over his chest while the other digs into his hair.

He nods. "I'm sure Liam and I can find time to babysit for that." He promises, his nose coming down to nuzzle Gianna's.

Liam sighs a little, seeming less than thrilled by the idea of a shopping spree and I'm somewhat relieved to see there is at least one thing this man and I don't have a shared interest in. It was getting a little too uncanny that he liked *everything* I did.

He pulls the bags out of the back of the car and Gabriel does the same for him and Gia. I'm a little surprised that they don't have all that much that they are bringing with them. I don't know what kind of *business* they are getting up to in Monaco, but I definitely expected them to need a lot more supplies to do it.

Gianna takes her bag and starts to head through the parking lot and Liam does the same. I go to follow but Gabriel grabs me around the forearm and pulls me back between the cars. If Liam or Gia notice, neither of them say anything.

"I need to make something clear to you." Gabriel growls. "I know Liam has this infatuation with you, and since he's my best friend I've been letting him take the lead on this. But the second you become a liability I will leave you with your throat slit in an alley."

I swallow, staring at him with wide eyes and nod numbly not knowing how else to react to that.

"Understood?" He asks.

"Yes." I rush out quickly, not wanting to get on his bad side.

He claps a hand on my shoulder. "Great." Gabriel smiles and that's somehow so much worse. "Grab your bag and let's go."

I do blindly as I'm told running after Liam very much realizing he's definitely the lesser of two evils. He smiles back at me and that smile doesn't make me want to throw up my coffee.

Liam snakes his free hand around the small of my back. "What did Gabriel say?"

I shake my head. "Nothing."

"That bad?" Liam asks, turning to briefly look back at his friend.

"I'll be fine." I assure him quickly. I don't think Liam would take what Gabriel said particularly well and I'm not trying to start problems between the two of them because that sounds like it would only end badly for me.

Liam doesn't seem like he believes me, but he just keeps walking along towards the terminal. He guides me through the several areas of nice lounge seating that no one is using towards one of the hangers on the far side. It's so much quieter than flying commercial and no one has stopped us to ask absolutely any questions or check any of our luggage. We just breeze through to the hanger where a rather large private jet is sitting.

A woman smiling warmly greets everyone by name including me which I'm surprised by because that means there is likely some kind of record of me being here. She takes the bags from us and begins to load them under the plane.

Liam takes my hand and leads me up the stairs and into the aircraft that is way more massive than is necessary for four people.

All of the seating is made out of white leather and the interior is lined with gold accents. A table that can seat four, two on each side is off to the left with a couch that can seat three facing it. Behind that is six more large comfortable looking chairs, two rows facing each other of two on one side and one on the other.

"Wine." Gianna says to the woman who took the bags. "Whenever you have a second."

The woman nods and heads off into the back.

Liam leads me to the table, pulling my laptop and his out of the computer bag he has slung across his shoulder. He put mine on the inside by the window, probably just as much so I can't leave as so I can look at the view.

I just slide in and start to open up the novella I'm working on. I'm perfectly content to spend however long this flight is zoning out and typing.

The flight attendant comes back with four glasses and a bottle of wine. She pours one and hands it to Gia and Gia proceeds to shove it into my hand but as fast as she does Liam takes it back away.

"She can't drink with what I have her on." He tells Gia, passing her back the glass.

Gia frowns a little but shrugs. "More for me I suppose." She takes a sip. "You need to put her on something else though so I can drink with my bestie."

"I haven't had to give it to her in a few days, but this is the first time she's been in public, better safe than sorry." Liam says. "As long as she behaves she can drink with you tomor-row."

I try to overlook the *behaves* comment and turn back to my laptop, hoping to lose myself in being antisocial.

Gianna huffs, but Gabriel waves her off. "He's right, and precautions are good, Gia." He says it in a way that very much makes me feel like it's not the first time they've had similar discussions about me.

She then proceeds to say something in what I assume is Italian that I don't understand. Her and Gabriel have some kind of conversa-tion that ends with Gia downing the rest of her wine and saying the one Italian word I do know. "Move!" She waves a hand at both the men. "Riley and I have had enough of your bullshit, we are going to sit in the back."

I'm not particularly sure I want to be dragged into this, but Liam and Gabriel do both move aside and Gia pulls me towards the two single seats on the side glaring at her husband as she does.

"Testa di cazzo." She mutters. "That one means dickhead."

I chuckle with a nod. "You're gonna have to say it slower."

"Testa. Di. Cazzo." She enunciates each word and I repeat them back to her. "Very good. Now yell it at my husband."

The threat Gabriel made flashes through my mind. "No." I say quickly. "I'd rather keep breathing, thank you."

Gianna scoffs. "Coward."

I cross my arms over my chest. "I am not a coward. I'm just smart enough to know when someone can and *will* kill me."

"He's not as scary as he looks." Gia says, but as I glance back at Gabriel, who's now started talking to Liam in Italian, that doesn't really feel true. Gianna doesn't push though, instead she changes the subject. "So how is the sex?"

I choke on air and my coughing draws Liam's attention. He's about to come check on me when Gianna waves him away.

"She's fine, I got her." Gia gives him a look that clearly says *sit the fuck back down* and pats me on the back softly. "So?" She insists. "How is it?"

"Gia!" I blush, giving her an incredulous look before glancing back over my shoulder at Liam. He did sit back down, but he is glancing over his shoulder intermittently to check on me.

"Oh just tell me!" Gia pushes. "I was the one who finally got you laid!"

I turn back to her and lower my voice. "He's not been as... aggressive as I was expecting." I say softly before peering over my shoulder to check if he's listening. Liam seems distracted now and the plane has turned on and started to taxi.

"Fasten your seat belts and prepare for take off." Comes over the loudspeaker. I do as instructed and everyone else does the same.

"Aggressive how?" Gianna asks at a volume that's way louder than I'm comfortable with.

I sigh. "He made a lot of threats about weapons play and hasn't followed through on any of them." I say chewing softly on my lip and trying to fight the urge to keep staring at Liam.

"Maybe he's waiting for you to be more comfortable with him." Gia suggests. "Weapons play requires a lot of trust. He might just not want to take things too fast."

I scoff at that. "If he didn't want to take things too fast he wouldn't have already moved all my stuff into his place and demanded I marry him."

"Oh good so he told you!" Gia smiles. "Did he tell you about the place I picked out in Paris to look at dresses? They offer free cake and champagne! It will be perfect."

My stomach drops a little. "Gia, I can't marry him."

Her face immediately sours. "Is his cock small?"

I gasp at her question. "No." I answer with a chuckle. "It's just... too fast. Even if we met in a more traditional way I don't know if I would ever meet someone and marry them within a year, let alone less than six months."

"Why not? Getting married is fun." Gianna says. "And you can always get divorced."

I take another look over my shoulder, "Somehow I have a feeling with Liam, that's not an option."

Chapter Thirteen

Liam

I managed to get Riley up to the suite without her trying to alert anyone for help or run away. I heard the threat Gabriel made, even though I pretended I didn't and it seemed to put the fear of god in her. Honestly that's good for me though, it makes me look like the good guy and Gabriel can be the hammer.

We are in the nicest suite that the hotel in Monte Carlo has. I guide Riley back into the smaller bedroom, putting our bags up against the floor to ceiling windows that look out onto the city. The mountains span the left side, stretching across the landscape before dipping into the sea that seems to go on infinitely to the right. The view is beautiful and I catch Riley stopping to stare out at it as she sits down on the white comforter.

A rug is stretched out under the bed with a pattern of blue and white lines going up and down it. A small navy dresser sits across from the bed Riley is stretched out on with a TV positioned above it. I toss my laptop bag onto the black desk between the bed and the window, knowing full well I'll move all my shit to the dining room later.

Riley's eyes start to droop like she's tired, but she doesn't tear her gaze away from the windows. She crosses one leg over the other, taking a breath like she's trying to make heads or tails of what's happening around her before collapsing backwards onto the bed.

I sit down next to her, brushing some of her hair out of where it's stuck in her glasses. I don't bother to ask if she's okay, I know she's not. This has been a lot for her and I'm sure she's overwhelmed. "You brought a swimsuit, right?" I ask, already knowing the answer.

"Yeah." Riley says.

"You could go get in the infinity pool for a little bit with Gia." I suggest, hoping I can find some distraction for her while Gabriel and I go take care of some things. It's still way too early in the day for her to go to sleep, even though it seems like she might want to.

She pushes herself up a little so she's sitting on her elbows. "There are lounge chairs out there, I could go write more."

I nod. "That's always an option."

Riley looks at me like she's examining me, "But not an option you'd suggest?" She questions, seeming to sense that I was hoping she would actually take a little time to herself away from her laptop.

"Everyone needs a break, Riley." I tell her softly. "In another couple hours you can drink with Gia and the pool is heated. Doesn't it sound nice to sit in the water and look out at that view?" Honestly I'm being a little selfish too, I know if she's with Gianna that Gia will keep an eye on her. Even if Gia is being the most lax out of the three of us, she still won't let Riley run off.

I don't have any contingencies in this suite besides the camera I'm going to set up at the door with a motion detector. It's the first time I'm going to have to leave her since I've taken her somewhere she can actually escape from and I'm more than a little nervous she'll take the opportunity.

If she gets out into the streets of Monaco on her own I have no idea what she'll do. Would she just try to figure out a way back home? Would she try to hide from me? Would she go to the police? Would she come back? I didn't want to find out the answer to any of those questions.

Riley sighs. "As much as I like Gia, we just spent like four hours together. I was kind of hoping for some time to write."

I'm being overprotective and I have several trackers on her, the one on her ankle she has no hope of getting off short of finding a pair of bolt cutters. Gia promised she'd stay with her in the suite even if they weren't hanging out so it should be fine. I just... I don't want to lose her.

I lean down and press a long kiss to her lips, one full of desperation and longing even with her right here next to me. "Please just... don't leave, Riley."

She scoffs. "Is that why you're being so extra?" She waves a hand around. "Liam, look at this place. Do you see that view? Did you see how nice that pool is on the terrace? I have my laptop and I'm in the best suite in all of Monaco. I'm not going anywhere as a matter of fact if Gia wants to go shopping with me, she's going to have to *drag* me out of here by my hair."

I chuckle, feeling a little reassured by that.

"So can you stop worrying?" She asks, running a hand through my hair.

"About you?" I shake my head. "Never. But I do feel slightly less anxious about you trying to run out of here the first chance you get."

Riley shrugs and that's less reassuring. "It would be easier to run from you in New York. I actually know how to get around there."

I press a kiss to her forehead. "I'll remember that."

I rifle through Louis Monreaux's cabinets, not really looking for anything, more just bored and wanting to know more about who I'm hunting. Lots of tea, some pantry staples, canned foods, dried premade pasta, which this close to Italy is basically a sin.

Gabriel took one of the bottles of whiskey from Monreaux's liquor cabinet and helped himself to a glass. He's currently sitting over on the couch, not having to busy himself with knowing his target because he knows I'll do that for him.

No, Gabriel's job is rather to look scary and with his gun sitting on his lap in his all black suit and a rocks glass, he definitely looks just that. You'd think, since I'm technically the muscle on this, my job would be to intimidate but my work is more about surveillance.

I've already installed a keylogger on every device of Monreaux's that I've been able to find. He's got a few cheap laptops, I have no way of knowing which one he uses. I also set up recording and screen mirroring software so anything he does will get broadcast untraceably back to me.

I then proceeded to spend twenty minutes bugging his place so we'd have ears on him at all times. The bugs I set up go in outlets so they use them as a powersource and unless someone is planning to change their wall fixtures anytime soon, they won't see them. The few I set up should pick up just about everything in the apartment with no issues.

"This whiskey is shit." Gabriel eyes it, kicking back the rest of his second glass. "I would have expected someone who pockets two hundred thousand a year and steals sports cars to have better booze."

I huff a laugh. "I wouldn't have. They are scraping by. They're in debt to someone." I close the cabinet I was looking through coming over to look out the windows at the brick wall he has a view of. "Probably pissed off the wrong person at some point and are still paying for it."

"They seem to have a habit of doing that." Gabriel observes, pouring himself another glass of whiskey despite calling it shit.

I had snuck into Corbin's place earlier today by myself to put the same kind of surveillance equipment in his apartment too, it was lower end than this one. They are making good money, it has to be going somewhere and it's not to living expenses.

We've been here about an hour at this point waiting, we knew that we'd be waiting though and came early on purpose. Monreaux and Corbin had a meeting today, likely with who they are in debt to, and were planning to come back here to talk privately after. At least that's what I picked up from their text conversations.

My French is a little rusty. Reading or understanding it I do okay, but trying to speak it is harder because I keep trying to dip into Italian, in this case that might not be a bad thing though. People know the Italians don't fuck around. If I accidentally slip in a wrong word it would probably work to my advantage.

The apartment is painted in white walls that look rather dirty like no one has cleaned them within the last year. The furniture reeks to the point where I didn't want to sit on it. Knowing Gabriel he'll take an hour long shower when we get back to the hotel to wash the feeling of grime off his skin.

Everything is all in one room except the bathroom and the bedroom. Our hotel suite is larger than this apartment. Hell, my bedroom back home is larger than this apartment.

The U shaped kitchen in the corner takes up about half the space and is connected to the small living room area with a single couch and two arm chairs. I saw the bedroom when I was bugging it and there is only a mattress on the floor with no sort of bed frame or anything. Surprisingly it did have sheets though.

I wish this window had a better view so I could see the hotel from here. I'm worried about Riley. I know Gia has her, I know she said she would stay, but I can't help the uneasy feeling in my stomach that I might get back and have her not be there.

If she left, Gia would call me or my door camera would go off. The only notification I got on the door sensor was when Gianna got the room service they ordered. Gianna was insisting before we left that they get pizza despite having dozens of fancy ass options to choose from. Riley just went with it because she didn't really care what they had as long as she didn't have to stop writing to have a discussion about it.

I hear the lock to the apartment starting to be fumbled with as well as some soft discussion outside the door and turn around to watch the fuckers come through the door. I keep my hand lightly on the gun strapped to my hip in case they are armed but most likely they aren't since they had to go meet with their creditors.

They come through the door wearing nice polos and slacks, likely not wanting to look too poor or too rich when meeting with people they owe money to. They are both roughly in their forties. Their hair is slicked back lightly in similar styles, but Corbin's is dirty blond and Monreaux's is brown. The pair is so deep in conversation that it takes a second for them to look up and see me and Gabriel in the apartment.

Now this conversation happened entirely in French, but I'll make this easier on you.

"Who the fuck are you!?" Jean Corbin just about screamed, his blue eyes going wide.

"Come in." Gabriel says, calmly like he owns the place as he quickly switches over to French when he hears them speak it, but he uses an accent that is a mix between Italian and American.

"Don't do anything stupid." I smile, leaning back against the window.

"Close the door." Gabriel orders. "Let's talk."

Corbin and Monreaux look between each other before glancing back at me in my black button up and look directly at the gun holstered at my side. Seeming to understand the other option was getting shot, they closed the door.

"Sit." Gabriel tells them, taking command of the room as he waves towards the chairs.

They do, knowing how this game is played. They just came from a meeting similar to this, they know how to act when a shark is in their midst.

"How was your trip to Venice?" Gabriel asks them. "Productive?"

Monreaux shakes his head. "I have no idea what you're talking about." He says, but the look of recognition flashes behind his eyes.

Gabriel takes a sip of their whiskey, seeming to want to draw out the tension in the room. I just cross my arms over my chest watching them with stern eyes and waiting for an order from Gabriel.

"You took something that belongs to some friends of mine." Gabriel says casually. "My friends don't like losing things." His hands goes to his gun. "How do you suppose we fix that?"

"We didn't know who's cars they were." Corbin rushes out.

Monreaux hisses at him. "Jean, shut the fuck up." He turns back to Gabriel. "You have the wrong men."

"Your buddy just said otherwise." Gabriel countered. "Those cars were expensive and I expect payment in money, cars, or blood, but I will be paid, gentlemen." Gabriel tilts his head to the side. "Where are my cars now?" He asks, already knowing the answer.

"We don't have them!" Corbin answers.

"Jean, stop fucking talking!" Monreaux barks.

"You're going to get us killed!" Corbin argues before turning back to Gabriel trying to reason with the man holding the gun. "Sir, we don't have your cars, but we can pay. Please we can pay."

Gabriel chuckles, looking to me. "They can pay." He says with a laugh. "Do you pieces of shit have any idea how much those cars are worth?" Gabriel cocks his gun. "Maybe it will be easier to just collect my debt in blood."

"No!" Monreaux begs. "He's right. We can pay. We... we have a tournament this Saturday." Gabriel lowers the gun slightly like he's listening. "The prize is two hundred thousand euros. We can get it for you. Please, that has to be enough for the cars."

"Louis, what about Laurent?" Corbin whispers.

"Fuck Laurent, we have bigger problems." Monreaux huffs. He's right, they do have bigger problems.

Gabriel shakes his head. "How do you know you'll get the money?" He challenges.

"We rig it." Monreaux admits. "Have been for the past five years. It works, I swear. We'll win the tournament, and get you the money please. But you have to let us live to win it."

Gabriel pretends to think about it for a second. "I think I can accept this type of payment. *In cash.*" He stresses. "But if I don't have the money by Sunday morning your bodies will be in the Mediterranean by noon. Do I make myself clear, boys?"

They both nod.

"Good." Gabriel smiles. He sets the glass down on the table. "And get better whiskey. This stuff is shit and I don't drink swill." Then he turns to me. "Let's go." Gabriel leaves without a second thought.

I walk to the door, turning around and smiling at them before I leave, "We'll be watching, fuckers." Then I slam the door behind me, hard.

Chapter Fourteen

Riley

We've been in Monaco for two days and I've spent all of it locked in this stupid beautiful prison. Gianna has asked Gabriel a few times if we can go out shopping but him and Liam have been too busy with other shit to take us. Apparently they don't trust me to go out with just Gia yet.

Liam and Gabriel are in the dining room gathered around the white marble table that Liam has covered in random electronics bullshit that I have no hopes of knowing what it all is. I've honestly just been trying to avoid going in there all together. Gabriel terrifies me. Plus the picture on the wall is creepy. It's two white dudes standing by a railing making very fake looking smiles with an ornate golden frame around it. I hate it, it feels like they are staring at me.

Gia and I are laying out beside the infinity pool. They have small lounge beds that are just a little mattress on a wooden plank, but are surprisingly comfortable. Gianna is soaking up the lasts of the sun and enjoying the view of the ocean while I'm typing on my laptop trying to get a few more words down for the day.

I've been distracted hanging out with her and have done very little writing so I'm only sitting at about thirty four thousand words. This project is going to turn out a lot longer than I was expecting.

Gia sighs, loud and exaggerated, "For fucks sake, put the laptop away." She rolls over to look at me. "You've been on it this whole fucking time."

"This is my job, Gia." I look up from the scene I'm writing.

She waves me off. "Who needs a job? Liam makes more than enough for you to live on. Your job should be hanging out with me."

"I like what I do." I tell her. "Writing makes me happy and it's good money with the following I have." Not that I've been able to keep in touch with that following since Liam is still holding my phone hostage. I do occasionally go off the grid though so hopefully my readers won't find my disappearance too weird.

"Is that why you've been scowling at your screen all day?" Gia asks, closing my laptop for me. "Because it makes you happy?" I glare at her but she just waves me off. "I need a drink."

"There's wine in the living room." I shrug. Between the two of us we've already gone through three bottles today. Liam decided I would be okay off the drugs since alcohol would slow me down too, I rolled my eyes when he said it, but at least I can drink.

Gianna shakes her head. "I want to go out for drinks. Monte Carlo is beautiful and we're trapped in a room!" She huffs, flopping onto her back and crossing her arms.

I look around at the terrace and honestly don't mind being stuck here that much. The infinity pool is rather big for the fact that it's on the roof of a building. There's a small garden on the other side of it down the steps. Plants litter the terrace, all well taken care of and flourishing.

There is a sitting area with gray patio furniture between the doors to the living room and the pool with three nice chairs and one long couch. A small round table sits in the corner that Gia and I have been eating at for the last two days since she didn't seem any more interested in trying to venture into the dining room than I was.

I roll over on the poolside bed, setting my laptop on one of the little gray hexagonal tables that sit beside me. "We could ask the guys." I suggest.

Gia scoffs. "Those bastards will just say no."

"Then I don't know what you want from me, Gia." I shrug.

She shoots up right excitedly, smirking at me deviously. "Let's sneak out!" She says, her voice full of excitement but her words quiet.

I shake my head. "Fuck no."

"Come on, it will be fun!" Gianna says.

I point down to my ankle. "Gia, Liam will know the second we leave the hotel."

"Then we don't leave the hotel." Gianna walks over to the phone mounted to the wall and dials a number on it. "Hello, room service?" She proceeds to order a bottle of wine and nothing else before coming to grab my hand and dragging me up from where I was sunning in comfort.

"We'll use the room service as an excuse to open the door and then slip downstairs to the hotel bar." Gianna whispers. "They're too distracted to notice that we ducked out when the room service arrived."

"Gia, this is a bad-" I was about to try and discourage her more when she opened the door to the living room. I shut up then because Liam and Gabriel are in the other room and would be able to hear us, but I try to implore her with my eyes that this is a bad plan.

She just drags me into the living room to sit down on one of the couches and starts chatting innocently like she's not planning our escape. "I think Gabriel and I need to have another child when you and Liam start trying. That way your baby will have someone to play with."

I try not to choke on that thought, but when Gia waits a second, looking towards the dining room to see if Gabriel will react I realize what she's doing. She's checking how much they are paying attention.

The living room is made up of two large tan sofas, one a three seater and the other an L shaped that could sit up to seven. The couches are covered with rectangular blue, red, and gold pillows. Two small red arm chairs sit across from the L shaped couch and under all of it is a red and blue rug that matches well with the pillows. A few small pear shaped tables are in the middle with different sweets a top them as well as random decor items.

Gia pushes back up off the couch and pokes her head into the dining room. "We ordered more wine." She purrs softly.

Gabriel just waves her off before coming up to her, turning her around, and pushing her out the door. He then proceeds to close the glass door behind her and go back to talking to Liam.

I chuckle and hate to say it but her plan actually isn't *that* bad. I know I shouldn't be going along with this, but she's right we've been stuck in this room since we got here and it might be nice to get out for a change. I don't have any plans of trying to run, not actually, but I'm going just a little stir crazy and drinks at the hotel bar sounds amazing.

What I said to Liam I meant. Running here would be way too hard. When we get back to New York, that's a different story, but at least while he has me trapped in Europe, I'm better off just going where he tells me. And I know that... so why am I letting Gia talk me into this?

There's a knock on the door a few minutes later and Gianna grabs me off the couch, forcing me into this mess with her.

She answers it and smiles, taking the bottle from the man. She looks at the label before calling back to him and following him into the hallway with me in tow behind her. "Wait! This bottle is no good." She shoves the bottle back at him. "Take this back, we don't want it."

"Of course, ma'am." The man says, his French accent heavy. "My apologies."

"We'll just go down to the bar." Gianna smiles. She rushes me down the hallway and into the elevator and the man takes off down a different hallway.

My heart is beating out of my chest as the elevator doors close and we somehow manage to actually get away with this. "Gia, if

Liam doesn't kill me Gabriel definitely fucking will."

She waves me off. "You'll be fine. I've snuck out loads of times when Gabriel has told me to stay put. This is a right of passage. You'll get used to it and then your face won't look like that next time."

I bristle. "Look like what?" I huff.

"Like a terrified shih tzu." She chuckles.

I'm about to rebuttal against that when I hear something beep. "What the fuck was that?" I hear it again and look down to see there's a light on my anklet I hadn't seen lit up before. "GIA!" I scream.

She grumbles. "William and his stupid tech. Fucking testa di cazzo." She shrugs and drags me off the elevator towards the sounds of soft piano music. "Too late now, best make the most of our ten minutes of freedom."

I glare at her as she pulls me into the hotel bar.

Everything in the place seems to be made of a dark cherry wood, the bartop, the walls, most of the chairs. Mirrors are spaced intermittently through the space as well as behind the bar. There are glass shelves lined with liquor bottles that Gia is bringing me towards.

She pushes me into one of the leather seats and waves a hand in the air to flag over the bartender.

He glares at her too, seeming to not like being summoned before asking, "What can I get for you, American?"

She scoffs, making sure to stress her Italian accent as she says, "Where is your wine menu?" He hands it to her and she looks over it briefly before pointing to one. "A bottle, four glasses."

"Expecting us?" Liam asks, coming up from behind us with a rather pissed looking Gabriel beside him.

"This wasn't my idea." I rush out.

Gabriel sighs. "Trust me, I know."

"I was dragged into this." I defend.

He waves me off. "You're spared for tonight, Riley, I know when something is my wife's doing."

I let out a relieved sigh.

"Don't relax just yet, love." Liam purrs in my ear. "I still have to punish you for your little jailbreak. It might not have been your idea, Riley, but you could have tried to warn us."

"I'm not a snitch." I say simply.

Gabriel huffs a laugh. "I knew there was a reason I liked you." And that might be the nicest thing he's said to me.

"Regardless." Liam comes to sit down beside me. "You're in trouble."

I run my hand down his front. "Maybe I can find other ways to serve my punishment." I purr seductively hoping I can maybe distract him instead.

He leans into me. "Unlikely."

I bristle and straighten as the man behind the bar returns with the bottle and four glasses. He pours Gia a taste and when she nods, he pours for everyone else.

Gabriel takes a sip of the wine and sighs. "How much is this bottle gonna cost me, Gia?"

"Eight thousand." She smirks and I try not to choke on the rather large sip of wine I took. Gabriel however seems a lot less phased.

"Better than that night in Moscow." He shrugs, drinking the wine like it's not two months rent for me. I'm honestly convinced that Gia just picked the most expensive bottle on the menu to piss Gabriel off. He then proceeds to lean into Gia and whisper something in Italian that I have absolutely no idea what it means. With how wide Gia's eyes go I'm pretty sure I don't want to know either.

"Gabriel." She says like she's trying to reason with him, but I quickly no longer have time to care when Liam turns my chair towards him.

"What were you thinking?" He asks.

"I..." I bite my lip trying to figure out how to answer that question. "I just wanted to get out of the suite for a little bit."

Liam leans into me. "Have you tried to ask anyone for help?" He asks so quietly even I almost don't hear it.

I shake my head. "No."

"Should I believe you?" He asks softly.

I nod quickly. "I didn't, I promise." I don't know if he believes me, but he doesn't question me further.

"Better take your time drinking that wine, love." Liam growls. "Because when you're done with your glass I'm taking you back up stairs and this time when I punish you, it will be a lot more than just a kiss."

My eyes go wide as I take a sip and swallow hard. Suddenly I feel like nursing my drink is a very good idea. Last time Liam punished me it very much felt like he was holding back, the look in his eyes makes it clear that will not be the case this time.

I run my finger around the rim of the too empty glass, cursing myself for drinking so much of it already even if I didn't know I needed to pace myself before this.

"Drink, Riley." Liam orders after a few minutes of a staring match between the two of us. He's more than half way through his own glass by this point and has spent this entire time staring into my soul or undressing me with his eyes.

I put the glass to my lips and take a small sip of it, feeling like I *have* to listen to him.

"Good girl." He purrs, his hand slipping to my knee. "More."

I nod and put the glass to my lips again, getting more than a little distracted by his hand on my leg and taking a much bigger sip than I planned.

Liam smiles and leans in. "Feel it yet?"

I look back and forth between him and the wine. I shake my head denying him. "I've... I've been right here the whole time. There's no way you..." But even as I'm trying to deny it, I can tell I'm starting to feel a little off. "What is your obsession with drugging me?"

He shrugs his hand, drifting further up my leg as he does. "It's fun."

"What is it?" I ask.

He shakes his head. "What it is, is a warning to watch your drink better, Riley." His hand moves under my skirt and his fingers brush against my pussy.

"That's not what I mean." I hiss, getting agitated that he keeps fucking spiking my shit and somehow I keep not noticing.

"I know what you mean." Liam says. "But I'm not telling you this time." He slips his hand under my panties and starts to finger me. "Finish your drink, Riley."

I glance over my shoulder and notice that Gabriel and Gianna have already disappeared to where I don't know. A quick slap to my pussy has me turning my attention back to the man whose hand is between my legs.

"Eyes on me, Riley." Liam orders.

I nod. "Yes, Sir." I reply quickly, feeling like that's what he wants to hear in this moment. I guessed correctly because Liam smiles.

"Finish the drink." He repeats.

I shake my head, the small part of my common sense remaining remembering that I'm getting in trouble the second this drink is done and he can drag me upstairs. Not to mention the survival instinct that's flaring to life inside of me telling me how bad of an idea it is to drink something I know has been tampered with.

"Finish it." He growls.

That survival instinct goes promptly out the window, seeming to realize the predator in front of me is a bigger problem than whatever drugs he's trying to slip me. I pick up the drink and kick the rest back like I was told to.

"Good." Liam grabs my hand and drags me away from the bar back towards the elevator. My feet struggle to keep up underneath of me, because I'm dragging on purpose or because of the drugs starting to take a hold I don't know, but Liam must notice because he sweeps me up into his arms and starts to carry me.

The elevator opens and he sets me back on my feet before hitting the button for the top floor. The doors close again and before I can process what's happening I'm pinned up against the wall and I feel something pressing into my side.

My eyes go wide as I realize he has a fucking gun and is holding it against me. "Liam."

I whimper out, feeling the adrenaline spike. "I'm sorry."

He nods. "Oh, you're going to be, love."

Everything is a haze as I'm shoved out of the elevator and Liam starts to chase me down the hallway as I scurry away from him closer towards the suite. My back hits the doors and he uses a keycard to open them before grabbing me by the hair and dragging me inside.

He's been rough with me when we've had sex before but it was nothing like this. His eyes glimmer with something ruthless, something terrifying.

As we come into the suite I vaguely hear a scream come from the other bedroom followed by a whimper and a moan. Clearly Gabriel has similar ideas on how to punish Gianna, but I don't have too long to focus on that because I'm being dragged through the living room.

I expect Liam to take me back to the bedroom, but he doesn't. He pulls me out onto the terrace and brings me in front of the pool.

"Strip, Riley." He orders, his voice rough and the gun still in his hand leaving no room for argument.

I pull my shirt quickly over my head before undoing my bra and tossing them both off to the side. I slip out of my panties and skirt but my eyes and squarely focuses on the gun, not able to pay attention to anything fucking else right now.

"That's a good girl." Liam purrs, pulling his own shirt over his head with one hand. "Get on your knees and crawl to me."

I drop like a rock, falling to all fours as quickly as I can and walking on my hands and knees towards him. My head is completely empty now, all I can focus on is the man in front of me and trying to survive whatever he's about to put me through.

"Oh good, so you do know how to listen." Liam huffs, pressing the tip of the gun to my lips. I whimper and I would have thought he ignored it if I wasn't eye level with his cock and hadn't seen it throb. "You just fucking choose not to."

I try to steady my breathing and remind myself that this man probably won't kill me but the fact that I had to qualify that statement with *probably* isn't really doing much to reassure me. I want to beg for my life but he has the barrel pressed to my lips.

"Open, Riley." He orders.

Gods fucking help me I do because what the fuck else are you supposed to do when your kidnapper has a gun pressed to you but obey? Even if it looks like you're seconds away from dying.

He slips it into my mouth and I'm just trying not to cry. "Suck it off like it's my cock."

I whirl my tongue around it blindly listening and feel the little hole that the bullet comes out of. I'm shaking, I know I am, I'm trying not to but I can't stop. The edge that the bullet comes out of is lifted and my tongue feels every single little bit of it before slipping back to the boxed off sides.

Tears slide down my face as I lick and suck, trying to be light because I've never shot a gun and have no fucking idea how sensitive they are or how easily they could fire.

Liam pulls the gun out from between my lips with a pop and the second it's away from me I let out a loud sob. His hand goes into my hair stroking it softly in complete contrast with what he just fucking did to me. "Good girl, Riley."

"Please don't kill me." I mutter out now that I no longer have a fucking gun in my mouth.

I look up at him with wide pleading eyes and just keep whispering, "Please don't kill me."

"Breathe." Liam sets the gun down on the small table by the couches on the terrace. "It's not loaded, Riley. I wouldn't actually put you at risk like that." He comes down to eye level with me, lifting my chin up to look at him. "But now you know how fucking scared I was when the alarm went off on my phone that you went out of range."

I nod blindly.

"You don't like feeling that kind of fear do you, Riley?" He asks and I shake my head. "I don't either." He tells me. "Don't fucking try to leave me again."

"I'm sorry." I whisper. "I'm sorry. I'm sorry."

But he doesn't accept my apology. "Get in the pool." Liam orders, pulling me to my feet and smacking me on the ass.

I do as I'm told my adrenaline still pumping so hard through my veins that I can't think straight, or maybe that's whatever he fucking drugged me with. I climb down the stairs into the pool. The water is warming and soothing, I want to lose myself in it, but my eyes are glued to Liam.

He's pulling off the rest of his clothing and following me in. I back away from him but he just prowls closer to me until I'm backed up against the corner of the blue pool wall. Liam grabs me by the hips and drags me over to the infinity edge of the pool that flows over into the garden. He bends me over the ledge and spreads my legs wide under the water.

I gasp trying to get my bearing as I feel his cock slide up and down my slit.

"Have you ever been fucked in a pool before, Riley?" Liam purrs in my ear before slowly starting to push inside of me.

I shake my head. "No, Sir."

"Well we're about to change that, aren't we, love?" There is a smile in Liam's voice I can hear without even looking at him.

I moan at the feeling of him sliding into me. My head kicks back and his hand, that's not holding my hips, fists in my hair pulling me towards him and away from the edge.

My head is clouding and I can't think straight. All I can do is feel. Feel the water rippling around me. Feel his cock sliding in and out of me. Feel my head hanging over the edge of the pool.

I don't know how much time passes while I stare out into the night sky, looking out at the mountains and sea beyond. Everything starts to blur together and time feels non existent anymore. My vision starts to haze before my eyes fully roll into the back of my head as pleasure racks through me.

"Liam." I moan out.

"Riley." He growls back, his voice feral but the sound is music to my ears. It fills my soul and completes me in a way I wish it didn't. Some part of me can't help but *need* him and not just primally like this either. Something in my being feels like it aches for him.

I've never felt the way I feel about him before. I've never cared about someone in this way. I don't know if I would call it love, at least not yet, but it can definitely get there.

Maybe I'm being delusional because my life just flashed before my eyes. Maybe it's the fact that I'm currently high on whatever the fuck Liam gave me earlier that has my head so fucked. But whatever it is, I want him. More than that, I need him.

What the fuck is this man doing to me?

He thrusts into me hard, sending both water and my chest tumbling over the side of the pool. My head hangs down as I let out a shriek. Liam pulls me back upright, a hand shooting over my mouth. "Shhh, if you scream someone might get the wrong idea and think you're in trouble."

I have half a mind to scream for that very fucking reason now that he mentions it, but I don't. Instead I nod and let him keep fucking me because honestly, I want him to.

Liam lets go of my mouth in favor of holding my hips so he can fuck me harder. He pulls me up and down in tandem with his movements and I can feel his cock starting to stiffen inside of me. After a few more moments he lets out a groan as he finishes inside of me, his cock twitching as he fills me with his cum.

He pulls me back to my feet and lifts me up around my hips. He starts to carry me inside. Peppering kisses to my body as he does.

"What about our clothes?" I ask, feeling very exposed as he walks me through the common areas towards our bedroom.

"We'll get them in the morning." Liam promises. "I only got an hour on the terrace in the coin flip."

I look at him confused.

"Gabriel and I flipped for who would get it for an hour and who would get it for the night when we were in the elevator going to get you and Gia. He won." Liam explained with a chuckle.

"That was an hour?"

He shakes his head. "More, but Gabriel can fucking deal with it." Liam proceeds to toss me onto the bed. "Now I have to deal with you. I don't think I'm done punishing you yet.

Chapter Fifteen

Liam

We decided not to leave anything up to chance. We may not know exactly *how* Monreaux and Corbin are rigging the game but I feel reasonably confident enough that I can figure it out on the fly. Which is why Daniel Blakely managed to score a seat at their table. Besides if I can't, at least I'll be there to keep an eye on them to make sure they don't get squirrely.

"Just don't touch anything." I tell Gabriel and he glares at me kind of annoyed. We would have sent him but I know a lot more about baccarat. "The arrow keys will let you flip through the cameras, it should just play my audio. Don't touch anything else. If you have any problems, get Riley."

Gabriel scoffs. "I think I'm better equipped to try and fix it than Riley."

"Riley spends ninety percent of her time on her laptop. She may not be a hacker but I've walked her through some basic fixes yesterday and she got the hang of them quick enough. Get Riley." I tell him. "Don't break my laptop." And I do mean physically. It's fully possible he would throw it against a wall.

He rolls his eyes. "Yeah, whatever." That's not reassuring for the fate of my computer. I did ask Riley to try and keep an eye out for Gabriel getting frustrated, but she's still terrified of him so I don't know if she'd actually come interject if she saw him struggling. Guess we'll find out.

I adjust my tie, hating how fucking tight it is. This is why I don't fucking wear suits, but Gabriel insisted on an all black one that matched what he wore when we shook down Monreaux and Corbin. I get it, it gives a sense of unity, but I still hate wearing it.

Gianna managed to convince Riley to put her laptop away for the day. The two of them have been outside on the terrace and I haven't been able to think straight. Did I mention Gianna also convinced Riley to take off her bikini so she would tan evenly? Yeah, I can't stop fucking looking out the windows and neither can Gabriel.

Her blonde hair is pulled up in a messy bun with little strands hanging down framing her face. She keeps intermittently putting on a light sunblock so she doesn't burn and watching her rub it into her skin instead of doing it myself is my own personal form of torture.

It's like the two of them were specifically plotting to get us back for the other night. They knew we would be too busy today to actually divulge in the distraction and wanted to fucking taunt us. If Riley smirks and winks at me through the window one more time I'm going to go fucking pin her down on that little poolside bed and make her scream so loud someone calls the authorities.

"Why couldn't this tournament have been something I like? Poker is much more dignified and then I wouldn't have to be stuck up here behind a fucking computer." Gabriel grumbles.

"It's Europe, they like baccarat." I shrug.

"I fucking hate it." Gabriel responds. "It's so damned boring, I don't know how you don't want to blow your brains out after a couple hands."

I sigh. "It's a game of luck. There's almost no skill involved and there's something beautiful in fucking with shit you can't control." I pull my jacket off the chair and start to put it on. "Life is too easy when you know what's going to happen." I glance out at Riley. "Sometimes it's fun to lose yourself in something you just have to hope for the best on."

Gabriel rolls his eyes. "Yeah, well, speak for yourself. Some of us actually value control."

"I value it." I argue. "That's why I know how precious it is when it's taken away, from myself and others."

"We're not talking about baccarat anymore." Gabriel huffs.

I shake my head. "No, not really."

"Well focus on baccarat." Gabriel grumbles. "This money might be enough for you to afford the wedding dress Gia is gonna help Riley pick out next week." He chuckles. "I saw the prices at the place she's going to. Your wallet is gonna hurt by the time we get back to the states."

"Oh god, don't remind me." My gaze goes back out the window to Riley. "She'll be worth it." I say more to myself than to him. I already picked out a ring. Honestly I've had it this whole trip.

"I hope you're right." Gabriel smiles at me softly like he's still not totally convinced. I know he's just looking out for me, and himself, but I want him to like Riley. We've been friends as far back as I can remember and maybe it shouldn't but it matters to me if him and Riley get along.

I pop the small earpiece in and put on the watch I've rigged as a listening device. None of it should set off any flags if I have to go through any type of security either. I have a way to turn off the signal on the watch temporarily and it's connected to the ear piece, if they check for transmission (which I doubt they will) I can just disable it.

"Win me some money." Gabriel says as I head out the door. "Maybe I can give it to Gia as a budget when we're in Paris."

I huff a laugh. "Doubtful."

The casino is right across from the hotel. The large building looks more like something for government officials than gambling. It's not as gaudy as the casinos in Vegas but it's still as grand. The teal blue roof looks worn and weathered, rising into a round dome with two small tan towers on both sides of it. The original facade is a warmer color than the parts that had clearly been added on later when they needed to expand. It's a very symmetrical tan building that has black stairs leading up to three sets of doors.

I head into the main entrance with the herd of other people going to enjoy the festivities for the night. As I enter there's several stone tan and red marble pillars that seem more like decoration than actual support beams. The floors are lined with a white and gray tile with a few black ones interspaced to form a design in the center of the atrium. Large red and golden dice are stacked on top of each other in a centerpiece that rises into the sky.

There's a French sign in front of the doors to the casino floor directing people that only tournament players will be allowed back until after five thirty. A lightly armed man stands beside the sign with a clipboard, checking IDs and waving people through.

I walk up to him and pass the man my ID, well Daniel's ID, without even having to be asked.

He looks at it for a moment pretending to scrutinize it, but the look in his eyes says he doesn't *really* care. "Have a nice evening, Mr. Blakely." He tells me, opening the door to let me inside.

I'm more than a little surprised they didn't at least try to pat me down, but apparently they aren't concerned about people coming into the tournament armed. That kind of makes me want to go back for my gun, all I brought was a knife. I expected to get frisked. Guess I'll make do.

I walk through the room of dazzling bright slot machines towards the golden archway that leads into the main room. I had been here last night to scope the place out to make sure I had a good idea of security and layout. I assumed they would have more for the tournament especially since they are required to keep that prize money in cash on hand, but apparently not.

Royal blue couches and armchairs are littered around the outside of the space of the main room with golden throw pillows on each one of them. Little tables sit in front of each grouping for cocktails. The bar is off to the left of the room in front of some older looking paintings of people in clothing that appears to be from the early nineteen hundreds.

Baccarat tables are in a circle in the middle of the room, each one facing out. Dealers sit in the center of the circle each at a table already and chatting with the players who have begun to arrive. I quickly find Corbin and Monreaux's table and take my seat.

Monreaux glares at me the second I sit down and Corbin's eyes instantly go wide with fear. I can see Monreaux fighting the urge to scowl at me but I just smile.

Again, this all happens in French, but I'll translate.

"Hello, gentleman." I greet them, glad there's no one else at the table yet.

"What the fuck are you doing here?" Monreaux hisses, apparently not as scared of me as he is of Gabriel. "We told you we would get you your money. What more do you want?"

I look at him confused. "What money?" I ask. "I'm just here to play baccarat." I turn to Corbin. "I'd like my buy-in, please."

Corbin stares at me for a second before starting to count out the twenty thousand that we start with.

"Jean, what the hell are you doing?" Monreaux hisses. "He can't play."

"He paid for the tournament." Corbin says, passing me the chips. "He walked in the front door. He must be on the list. I have to let him play."

Moreaux scowls. "Fucking... whatever. You're not going to win, mobster."

"Maybe not." I shrug. "But the money from this tournament will still buy my fiancee's wedding dress regardless of if I win it or you do."

"Congratulations." Monreaux says dryly. "I was going to use it for rent, but I guess that's not nearly as important as a white gown."

I fight my urge to tell him that by the end of tonight he won't need rent money as a server comes over to us with a smile on her face.

"Hello, gentleman, can I get you anything to drink?" She asks sweetly.

"Yes." I tell her. "Get me and my new friend some good whiskey. That way I can show him what some tastes like." I lean over to Monreaux. "Don't worry, this is on me, so that way you can try and afford that rent money."

I quickly figured out exactly how they were rigging the game. Corbin was stacking the deck in a pattern, a long one so no one would notice, but I noticed. I was able to pick it up and start winning more of the bets.

The top two players from each table will compete in the back room at the end of the night for the prize money. I managed to score second at my table, behind Monreaux, but if the deck is stacked the same way in the back-room as it is up here I feel confident I can take the money without having to steal the cash from their corpses later. I don't feel like risking getting the cash bloody, bloody money is so much work to clean, both literally and figuratively.

"How'd the game go?" Gabriel whispers in my earpiece.

"I think I can win the money." I say softly, lifting my glass to make it look like I'm taking a drink, and not a weirdo speaking into my watch.

"Good." Gabriel says. "Do it. I'd rather not have to take it from them. Cash is heavy."

I chuckle into my glass. "Agreed." I've been trying to focus on what I'm doing, but I'd be lying if I said my thoughts didn't keep wandering off. "How's Riley?"

"I'm fine." I hear her purr through the microphone and have to fight the smile off my face. "Gabriel put Gianna in time out because she tried to answer the door naked when room service brought us a new bottle of wine so I came to check on you."

I have a feeling that's distinctly not why Riley came to check on things, but she probably doesn't want to throw Gabriel under the bus.

"She got the microphone working finally." Gabriel huffed. "This shit has too many fucking buttons."

"The microphone only has one button." I mutter, trying not to roll my eyes.

I hear Riley laugh before rushing out, "Sorry."

"Yeah well I've got it now, so you can go tell Gia she's free to get back in the pool." Gabriel tells Riley.

"Good luck, Liam." Her voice is raspy like she intentionally leaned closer to the microphone and she sounds fucking amazing. Fuck, I know its only been a few hours but I miss her.

"Focus up, lover boy." Gabriel growls. "They're calling you back."

I follow the archway and further back into the casino. They bring us past a red room full of slot machines before letting us through a set of doors into a smaller tan room.

There is a singular orange baccarat table and nothing else. The room has a bunch of random paintings of horses that I thoroughly don't understand, but who fucking cares, that's not really important. It's dark out the windows that are covered in green and white striped curtains and there's an older man standing in the room beside Corbin who is sitting behind the table.

"Gentleman!" The man greets. "I'm Mr. Amato, so glad to have you here tonight." He waves to the man standing in the corner. "We'll have our friend here do a quick pat down and scan of each of you, then we can get this game started."

Mr. Amato's gray hair is closer to balding, his figure rounding out because of age or lifestyle. His brown eyes are harsh despite his generally friendly words.

I click the button on my watch so the signal goes dark as the man by the wall starts to pat down Monreaux beside me. I'm now grateful I didn't bring my gun.

He moves to me next asking me to spread and I do, because my knife is in my shoe and I saw he didn't check Monreaux's shoes. The man does a quick pat down, not checking too thoroughly before running a wand over me quickly and moving down the line. When he's done with everyone and puts the wand away I click the button again to turn my mic and earpiece back on.

"Thank you, gentleman." Mr. Amato says as the man who checked us all goes to stand by the door. "Lovely to have you all here tonight, but we just need to be safe." He gestures to the table. "Please take your seats."

I make sure to pick a spot next to Monreaux on purpose, knowing that having to look at the man shaking him down will throw him off his game. "Are you well, my friend?" I ask Monreaux.

He scowls at me. "Fine."

Mr. Amato smiles at us all. "You will start with the same amount of chips. Minimum bet is five hundred euros. We play through eight decks and at the end of eight decks whoever has the most chips will win the jackpot. Any questions?" When no one speaks up Mr. Amato nods. "Let the game begin."

Chapter Sixteen

Riley

I hear a frustrated growl coming from the dining room and really don't want to go investigate it but Liam asked me to do my best to try and keep Gabriel from shattering his laptop. "Everything okay?"

"Yes." He grits out hitting a few keys angrily before sighing. "No." He gestures to the screen. "I can't find the camera for the backroom in the casino's feed and Liam's shit has been down since he went in.

"They may not have one." I tell him, coming around the table to look at the laptop. Surprisingly he moves aside to let me. I flip through the cameras quickly before checking on the secondary page that Liam showed me but I don't see anything.

"I don't like this." Gabriel huffs. "It's been quiet for over fifteen minutes. His shit should have come back up by now. He wouldn't leave it down for this long."

"Maybe some kind of jammer?" I suggest, running quickly through a few of the troubleshooting things Liam taught me to see if I can get the audio back. Nothing works and the audio stays silent.

I press the button and lean into the microphone. "Liam, can you hear me?" I have no idea how he would answer that short of sending a flare, but it was worth a try. "If you can hear me, we can't hear you." There's no reply, not that I'm expecting one.

"Yeah, that's real fucking helpful." Gabriel growls. He pushes me aside and slams down on the talk button. "Fucker, pull out. We're dark up here and I have a bad feeling about this."

I just kind of look at him, not saying but definitely thinking, *yeah, cause that was better.* "Maybe you're overthinking it." Honestly I feel like I'm saying that more for my sake than his. If something happens to Liam I don't know what Gabriel plans on doing with me but I don't think I want to find out.

"I've been doing this a long time, Riley." Gabriel says. "When I have a bad feeling, I'm usually right." Gabriel grabs his gun off the table tucking it into the back of his waistband and just about storming out the door.

"Wait!" I shout after him. "Is this the best plan? What are you going to do?"

He just kind of glares at me. "I'm going to go get my best friend out of whatever bullshit he walked into since he wasn't thinking clearly because of a girl and then I'm gonna kill the fuckers who put him there. Do you have a problem with that?"

I bite my tongue from telling him that storming in there with a gun is a bad idea but Gianna apparently has been listening and didn't feel the same compulsion for self preservation.

"You're being an idiot." Gianna chides him. "Liam can handle himself. He's not helpless. You going and causing a commotion is only going to stir shit."

Their argument quickly moves over to Italian at which point I have no idea what they are saying and just watch them bounce back and forth like a tennis match. If I don't get away from Liam, I seriously need to consider learning to speak Italian. I'm tired of being left out of shit.

After a few minutes of them bickering I'm at my wits end and finally pipe up. "Can you please speak in English so I know what's happening with Liam?" It comes out more exasperated than I was hoping for but Gabriel looks at me and smiles.

"Why do you care?" He asks, not aggressively either. He's asking like he's checking my motives.

I bite my tongue and shake my head, not wanting to think that much about exactly *why* I care because that means putting to words feelings I'm trying to avoid. "I just want to know he's okay."

Gabriel eyes me for a second like he's trying to perform a human lie detector test. "Gianna says I should wait the full half hour before going to get him and that I'm probably overreacting anyways. I told her *nicely* to shove it up her ass."

Gianna scoffs. "Testa di cazzo." She mutters. "What he said is he wants to go get them both killed and leave us as widows stranded in Europe. And not even the good parts of

Europe. If you're gonna die like a fool, at least do it in Paris."

I'm going to glaze right over the fact that Gianna just more or less told me I would qualify as Liam's widow if he dies tonight, because I can't handle absolutely any of that concept. "Okay, let's take a breath."

They both glare at me.

"Do we know if Liam is in any danger right now?" I ask Gabriel, more as a means to try and calm him down than an actual question.

"We know nothing because of the stupid cameras not working." He growls. "I don't care what you women say, I'm going." And with that he storms out the doors of the suite.

"Pazzesco." Gianna huffs. "That one means crazy. Not exactly a swear but still good to know."

I nod.

She comes around to the dining table and sits down in the chair beside me. "Let us watch our husbands get themselves killed, uh?" She gestures to the monitor.

"He's not my husband." I mutter pulling up the cameras and flipping through them to follow Gabriel.

"After tonight he'll be fish food, if Gabriel doesn't get his head on straight." Gianna grumbles.

Gabriel's stride is more steady as he exits the hotel and moves onto the square. He walks across the way towards the casino and heads inside the opulent front entrance.

My nerves start to spike as I watch him walk through the building and head towards the back. I can feel myself shaking even though I'm trying not to. I run a hand through my hair. "Gods, why do I even fucking care?"

Gianna pulls her eyes away from the computer. She grabs my hand and pulls me up out of my seat. "Let's get a drink." She tells me. "I hear the casino has a nice bar." She heads back into the bedroom and comes back a second later with two holsters, tossing one at me. "Let me show you how to put this on."

I nod blindly and follow her instructions, lifting my dress and strapping it to my leg before putting one of the guns on the table inside.

"You ever shoot before?" She asks me.

I shake my head. "Nope."

"Then do your best to not have to." Gianna says. "We'll teach you how to work a gun when we get back home. You need to know how to survive in this life, but for now." She walks me through the baseline mechanics explaining recoil and how to aim. "Don't try to shoot someone close to someone you don't want to shoot. You don't have the skills for that. Only life or death."

I nod because I don't know what fucking else to do. I'm more than a little surprised she is willing to give me a gun considering I am technically their hostage, but I guess they really don't treat me like one.

Gianna picks up her purse off the table before grabbing my hand and starting to drag me out the door. "Let's go check on our dumbass husbands."

"Two glasses of your most expensive red." Gianna tells the bartender behind the gaudy blue bar in the casino. "I'm punishing my husband's bank account."

The bartender nods and begins to pour two glasses, passing one to each of us.

Gabriel is around here somewhere, but neither of us have seen him. I don't know where he's snuck off to but there's no commotion near the backroom so he must not have tried to get in yet. Everything very much feels like the calm before the storm... well if you can call a casino calm.

The dinging and buzzing of slot machines fills the air. There are many tables of people chatting loudly and drinking way too much for my comfort. People loiter around in the seating areas laughing, lost in long conversations.

The bright lights are warm but still overwhelming not to mention the constant flashing of the machines. It's distinctly different from any casinos I've been to in the U.S. stylistically, but in essence they are more or less the same.

The gun strapped to my thigh is weighing my leg down, more because of the thought of it than the actual mass, as I stand next to a mob boss's wife in a casino in fucking Monaco and question how the absolute hell I got here. I have gone well beyond the dictionary definition of underqualified and straight into fraud.

"Gianna, I can't do this." I tell her as she sips her red wine casually like this is the most normal thing in the world. "Can't we just go back up to the room and wait for Liam and Gabriel to come back." I almost want to punch myself for *wanting* to go back to the cage Liam has locked me in, but I do, I really fucking do. I'm so far out of my depth I feel like I'm drowning.

"My best friend is no coward!" Gianna says passionately. "We will find our husbands, save their asses from whatever the hell bullshit they got into, and then make them pay for not taking us shopping the whole time we've been here."

I snort a laugh. "Gia, I can't save anyone. I have no idea what I'm doing, I don't belong here." And looking down at my green plaid skirt and sunflower crop top I feel very under-dressed.

She just waves me off, grabbing my hand and tugging me along. "Let's go play the slots." Gianna pulls me further into the casino into a room full of red and plops me down into one of the slot machine chairs that faces the door to the backroom that I know Liam is in.

Her and I spend roughly the next half hour playing on the machines and pretending like we aren't watching the door. There is still no sign of Gabriel and somehow that feels more ominous than him looming in the corner.

I have no idea where the fuck he disappeared to until I see him carrying a glass of whiskey and stumbling towards the guard infront of them room. Based on context, I can infer that he's not actually the drunk patron he wants to be seen as but I wouldn't have known that had I not known who he was.

Gabriel slams into the security guard with what I believe is an apology but I'm not entirely sure since he said it in Italian. He spilled the drink onto the man in the collision. The man just grumbles and shoes Gabriel back away from the doors. As Gabriel turns around he sees me and comes hurtling over.

"What the fuck are you–" He doesn't finish his thought before he sees Gia next to me and sighs. "Of course this is your idea. I should have fucking known. Go back to the suite. I've got it covered."

"Like fuck I will." Gia huffs. "What was your plan? Stain his shirt?"

Gabriel rolls his eyes and nods back to the guard who is now walking away from his post. "Guess who's going to go change now. I heard him radio for a new guard to swap as he was walking away which gives me enough time to get inside since he left the door un-manned."

I scoff, realizing how bad that idea is.

"Did you have something to say?" Gabriel growls at me.

I don't know where my backbone comes from. Maybe it's because I'm done being pushed around, Maybe it's because I don't want Liam to get hurt. Or maybe it's the gun strapped to my thigh but I straighten my spine.

"Yeah actually." I say and he eyes me. "What's your plan once you get in? Shoot everybody and then flee? There's probably more security in that room, do you think they are going to take very kindly to you barging in?"

Gabriel scowls. "I was going to pretend to stumble in looking for the bathroom and that would give me an excuse to check on him."

"That's a bad plan." Gia says with an eye roll.

"I don't recall asking either of you." Gabriel levels us with a glare. "Go back to the suite." But before he can turn around and execute his hairbrained scheme, another guard is already standing in front of the door. "Fucking great."

"Looks like you'll be stuck playing the waiting game with us." Gianna purrs, patting the chair of the slot machine beside her. "Take a seat, mi amore."

Chapter Seventeen

Liam

I have no idea what the fuck happened to my earpiece, but sporadically I'm getting laced with static and I haven't heard anything from Gabriel since before the game started. My suspicion is they have some kind of jammer since they thought to check for this kind shit in the first place, it's not that much of a stretch.

We have only a few cards left and I'm up by a lot. It's going to take a miracle for anyone else to catch up. Turns out Monreaux's memory is worse than mine, he keeps intermittently fucking up the pattern and isn't able to keep up. I can tell it's that too and not that he's just trying to throw a few hands to not seem too suspicious like I've been doing. His bets are too big for them to be intentional throw aways.

Corbin calls for bets and I drop a few chips on banker, knowing player will win. I'm doing my best not to get caught cheating. Monreaux places his bet on tie, forgetting that tie is actually the *next* hand. He places a big bet too, likely trying to recoup some of what he's lost.

The other players toss down bets of varying sizes, most of them realizing by this point that winning is probably a lost cause. The closest to me is Monreaux and he just threw away five grand on this hand.

Corbin closes the bets and starts flipping over the cards. I see the light scowl on his face as he's doing so, even though he's trying to stay professional. He must also know that Monreaux is about to lose this hand.

He flips over an ace and an eight for the player then a jack and a three for the banker, a natural win against crap. Corbin takes the banker and tie bets before cashing back out the people who bet on player. Those who just won get a little bit of optimism back in their eyes that I will be snuffing the fuck out like I will with Corbin and Monreaux later.

"Next round of bets." Corbin calls.

Monreaux scowls and tries betting on player with only a couple grand this time.

I wait for him to place his bet so he can't fucking copy me before smiling and putting down his exact bet from the round before. I set five grand worth of chips on tie and I chuck an extra three on banker pair just for the fuck of it.

Corbin draws the next round of cards once bets are closed, player ends up with a ten and an eight, banker gets two fours, and me? I get an ass load of chips.

The next few hands play on and I throw a couple intermittently but my thoughts are drawn away to Riley. I have no way of knowing what's happening with her right now since the earpiece is down and I really want to check on her.

I don't like leaving her for this long. She needs me to keep an eye on her. I don't trust Gia not to get her into some bullshit. The other night was bad enough. Maybe I'm being a little possessive, but she's mine so I'm allowed to be possessive.

The one night I woke up, half dazed and asleep, and when I reached over to pull her into me, she wasn't there. I just about had a fucking heart attack before I heard the bathroom door open and she came to slip back under the covers next to me.

Even a few seconds is too long for her to be separated from me. This has been hours. I'm more than ready to get back to her. I wish I didn't have to fucking work tonight. Especially since I'm going to have to dump bodies later and that's such a fucking hassle.

The last hand turns over and Corbin cashes out my winning bets. The men from the casino pretend to count how much each of the players has but it's clear that I've won.

Amato shakes my hand. "Congratulations, Mr. Blakely." He smiles. "The rest of you are dismissed, we must talk winnings."

Everyone but Amato and Corbin leave, including a scowling Monreaux. I can see the temptation in his eyes to scream that I cheated, which I did, but he knows that if he rats me out that it's the end of his scheme and he still believes he's going to live through the night.

"You did quite well for yourself." Amato chortles, coming to sit down in the chair beside me that Monreaux had vacated. "Had you been playing at a regular table you'd be walking away with half my vault."

I shrug. "Perhaps luck was on my side. My fiancee wants an expensive wedding." Not entirely true, I have a feeling Riley will be happy with something small, but it's the kind of bullshit thing you say when you win two hundred thousand.

"Ah then maybe you haven't made out quite as well as you need to." Amato chuckles. "Women will cost you. My first wife spent so much on our wedding I had to take a loan from my father. A big one. Maybe that's why god was on your side tonight. I've never seen someone win so much."

He's questioning if I cheated, I know he is. This is a game of odds and even though I made sure I took the occasional loss to offset how much I was gaining it was still enough to raise suspicion.

"If god had a hand in it he did it for my fiancee. He's always liked her more than me." I tell him. "But I just believe in good karma."

He nods. He has no way to prove I didn't win earnestly, if he did we wouldn't be having this conversation. Besides, admitting that I found out *how* to cheat in his high stakes tournament would look rather bad on his casino. His best option is to sweep this under the rug, give me my money, and hope I don't come back.

"Let's work out the finances then, yeah?" Amato says.

We spend the next few minutes talking about the taxes and all of the legal crap that comes with winning that much money. I then proceed to give him the information for a bank account in Daniel Blakely's name to transfer the money into. It's a joint account already setup with Mrs. Blakely. I have a card and ID for Riley to take with her when she goes dress shopping.

"Pleasure to have you in my casino, Mr. Blakely. Will you be testing your luck with any of our other games tonight?" Amato asks, his tone a little stilted.

"No, I have other business to attend to." I look over to Corbin with a smile.

Corbin visibly swallows before painting his face back into neutrality.

Amato on the other hand just about sighs with relief. "Then let me walk you out." Amato says, waving me towards the door.

As he guides me out of the room I catch a glimpse of Riley sitting at a slot machine and have to actively fight the urge to stop in my tracks. She smiles at me with Gianna and Gabriel sitting next to her also watching me.

I try to calm myself since at least she isn't in here alone. I let Amato lead me back out of the casino and check behind myself to see Gabriel following with Gianna and Riley in tow.

Politely I give my goodbyes to Amato and wait until the four of us get into the hotel to grab Riley by the wrist. I drag her towards the elevator with a soft, "What the fuck were you three thinking?" To which Gabriel fucking snarls at me.

"I was coming to check on you." Gabriel growls out as we get into the elevator. "What these two were thinking? I have no fucking idea."

Gianna huffs. "I was trying to stop my husband from getting himself killed!" She shoots a glare at Gabriel.

I go to guide Riley out of the elevator and as I do I feel a gun strapped to her thigh. My eyes go wide and I snatch it from her immediately, as I push her towards the suite. "Where the hell did you get this?" I growl in her ear.

"Gia." She whimpers, just about running away from me towards the suite.

Gabriel grabs Gianna's wrist dragging her into the suite after scanning the card. "You gave her a fucking gun? Gia, what the actual fuck?" He seems more pissed off than I am, which is saying something because I'm fucking fuming.

"She was fine!" Gianna argues. "She didn't shoot either of you and if I was her I would have." She crosses her arms over her chest. "I didn't know what we were going to be walking into."

"Speaking of which," I say, "Why did any of you come walk into that?" We move into the dining room and I start taking off the suit jacket and tie since I won't be needing it for the rest of tonight.

"Your audio went dark." Gabriel says. "I had a bad feeling, I was going to check on you. Apparently they had the same idea."

I sigh. "I was fine."

"I did try to tell him that." Riley mutters and everyone turns to glare at her. "I'll shut up now." She grabs Gia's hand and drags her towards the living room. "Let's go finish that bottle of wine."

Gianna follows after her as I start strapping a small arsenal under my clothing. We got the money, no one did anything stupid at the casino, Riley is safe, it's fine, I'm moving on. We have shit to do tonight.

Monreaux and Corbin come into the apartment in a rush. "What the fuck are we going to do? We don't have anything to pay them with now?"

"We need to run." Monreaux hisses, slamming the door behind him and not yet seeing me and Gabriel pressed up against the wall behind it.

"Run where, Louis?" Corbin asks. "Where can we go that they won't find us? Not to mention Laurent jumping down our throats. If they don't find us-"

We leap out in tandem, I grab Monreaux and Gabriel grabs Corbin. He tries to elbow me on instinct but I stand strong. I quickly pin him against my front, bringing my knife up to his neck. Before he can really process what is happening or struggle further I run my knife across his throat. Knives are a lot quieter than a gun.

I toss him to the ground as he sputters trying to gain oxygen. I kick him onto his side so I can check that he's actually dead, but it doesn't take long with the incision I made. His breathing comes to a stop and his eyes gloss over.

I look over to Gabriel to see Corbin on the ground at his feet, his hair covered in blood from how he fell to the tarp we have covering the carpet. We work fast, I'm not surprised they didn't see us and couldn't put up a fight.

Gabriel wiped his knife off on Corbin's shirt before tucking it back in his boot. "Idiots." He mutters. "Stealing from the family and then being stupid enough to not watch their backs."

I nod.

I'll spare you the gory parts but the end result is us packing their bodies in parts into duffle bags and lowering them out the window to the alleyway between the buildings. Typically Gabriel and I wouldn't dispose of the bodies ourselves, but since it's just the two of us we have no one else to shaft the work onto.

We've done it enough times that we know what we are doing but that doesn't mean it's fun. In our younger years Gabriel's father made us dispose of the bodies from our first job ourselves to make sure we knew how to.

Silently we load the bags into the back of the plastic lined rental car and bring them to the section of the beach we scouted out. At this time of night there's no one here so it's easy enough to tie weights to the bags and toss them into the water off the pier, letting half of our problem sink away into the Mediterranean.

Chapter Eighteen

Riley

Liam chewed me out for letting Gianna strap a gun to my leg and then proceeded to show me the small leather paddle he brought with "just in case" and spanked me with it until I was screaming so loud that Gabriel yelled at him to gag me or stop. Gabriel coming to my rescue was the furthest thing from what I was expecting to happen, but I was thankful, until Liam did pull out a fucking gag and keep going.

I shift in the luxury seat at the table on Gabriel and Gia's private jet, trying not to think about how much my ass hurts. I can see Liam smirking as I hiss with the movement and I'm sure he's pretty damn proud of himself.

"Stop that." I glare at him.

He shrugs. "No idea what you mean, love."

"You're so full of shit." I mutter, trying to focus on what I'm writing but my attention is more on him. He keeps pretending to be working and then casually slipping his hand up my skirt to touch my thigh.

Gianna and Gabriel are in the seats behind us, mostly on their phones or chatting about their kids. Intermittently their conversation slips into Italian, but I'm not really paying much attention to it.

The flight to Paris is short enough but I still wanted to try and write. Liam closes his laptop before saving my document and closing mine too. His hand slips back up my skirt and this time he doesn't just leave it on my thigh.

I bite my lip and fight the urge to check over my shoulder to see if we are being watched as his fingers skim over my pussy. He took my underwear this morning before we left and put them in his pocket promising to *give them back later if I behaved.* I had a very strong feeling that wasn't going to happen though, my panties much like my phone will probably remain confiscated indefinitely.

Liam's fingers find my clit and start to rub against it softly as his arm that's closer to me wraps around me and pulls me into him. "Don't moan." He whispers in my ear.

I nod as he starts to knead my clit with more pressure. I take a breath trying to stabilize myself and turn my head to look out the window. The light blue sky and the fluffy clouds look beautiful but I can't even slightly focus on them right now.

"Wanna join the mile high club, love?" Liam purrs, his fingers slipping inside of me and starting to make soft strokes.

Fighting the moan is a hell of a lot harder now. "Yes, Sir." I respond quickly. Mile high club is absolutely a bucket list item for me, one I never thought I would accomplish before Liam came into my life.

Two fingers curl inside of me, causing me to bite down on my lip so hard it fucking hurts to keep from moaning his name like I want to. This is some form of torture and he's doing it to me on purpose, I just fucking know he is. The fucker is diabolical.

I turn to look at him and see the shimmer in his eyes as he watches my face like he's just waiting for me to break and start moaning.

I don't think Gabriel and Gia would care that much, but I'd still prefer for them not to know Liam is over here fucking me with his fingers.

"I want you to finish on my fingers." Liam orders softly.

My eyes go wide. "I can't do that without..." I whisper back to him, imploring him with my eyes about how much that I would not be able to stay silent if he made that happen.

"I don't care, Riley." Liam growls, his thumb working my center harder as his fingers start to move faster. All of it feels like the perfect storm brewing between my legs and I have no concept of how much time has passed but I know I'm getting close. "They don't either. Do as you were told."

I pull my hand up to my mouth to silence the whimper that was trying to slip from my lips. I bite the back of my hand trying to calm myself with the pain but it doesn't fucking work. I feel him bringing me to the edge and know I'm about to topple over.

Liam turns my head towards him with the hand not between my legs and pressed a kiss to my lips. It feels like he's trying to swallow me whole as he roughly kisses me, way deeper than I was expecting him to. His tongue slides between my lips and starts to dance with my own.

I gasp as my orgasm washes over me and do my best to finish as quietly as possible, but with the way Liam is touching me that's almost fucking impossible. I feel like my mind is melting, like my world is shattering and tilting on its axis and right then the whole plane rattles with turbulence, shaking my still sore body and jolting me closer to him.

Liam waits a second for the turbulence to stop before grabbing my hand and pulling me up from the seat. He drags me past Gabriel and Gia towards the back.

Gabriel rolls his eyes. "Could have done without the PDA." He mutters.

Gianna slaps him on the shoulder. "Let them be young and in love you fucking old sourpuss. You never touch me like that anymore." She huffs.

Gabriel looks at her incredulously and the last thing I see before Liam drags me into the bathroom is Gabriel's hand sliding up Gia's skirt.

I'm quickly too busy to think about that because Liam is pinning me up against the bathroom wall and hiking up my skirt. The bathroom is bigger than one on a commercial plane, but not by a lot.

Liam undoes the zipper on his jeans and pulls his pants down enough to get his cock out. He grabs me around the center lifting me up and against the wall before slowly starting to lower me onto him.

I moan then, my head kicking back as I feel him fill me deeply. Right as he seats me fully on him the whole plane shakes and us with it. Liam does his best to balance but my head hits up against the wall behind me and I gasp.

"You okay?" He asks softly, the hand on the arm not holding me up going to my head.

I nod. "I'm okay." I promise. "Keep going."

Liam doesn't move again until he's thoroughly felt my head to make sure for himself that I'm okay. Once he's satisfied with his check he begins to bounce me up and down on him softly.

"Fuck." I mutter, as he slams me down on him so hard my eyes roll into the back of my head. "Liam."

He pins me between himself and the wall, holding me up with his arms as he starts to drill into me in a more consistent rhythm. The whole plane shakes around us as the turbulence hits again.

I gasp, grabbing at him desperately trying to keep steady as the floor rattles beneath us. My heart is racing in my chest, my breath coming out ragged and harsh.

"I've got you, love." Liam promises and for whatever stupid fucking reason, I trust him. He means it. I know he does and I know I shouldn't believe him but I do.

"Liam." I moan, my voice full of need that I so fucking wish was just physical but it's starting to go beyond that. I'm not sure I know how to cope with that beyond just letting myself fall into him.

The plane dips and so does my stomach as I grip his shoulders hard. Liam somehow manages to stay steady, manages to keep fucking me like everything isn't moving around us and it's damn impressive. He's damn impressive.

Holy fuck, am I falling for my stalker? My kidnapper? I'm fucking insane, but suddenly he hits that spot inside of me that has me moaning and I'm not sure I care anymore. Maybe being sane is overrated.

The dick can't possibly be that good can it? To warrant a complete abandonment of my sanity? There's no way anyone is that fucking good. Then his lips find my neck.

Liam bites down softly before starting to suck the tender flesh into his mouth. My head tilts to the side to give him better access to me and he sucks harder. I can feel the area starting to get hot under his lips and I have to focus on my breathing just to keep from losing it on the damned spot.

I don't know how much time passes before he pulls away but when I look at myself past him in the mirror behind us I see that the hickey he left is dark fucking red and purple. He licks across it and I shudder with how sore the area is.

His lips press to mine then and as I lick them they almost taste coppery, like he sucked on my neck hard enough to get a little blood. Fucking psycho. But then why do I want him to do it again on the other side? Gods, I think I'm obsessed with him.

I tilt my head the other way and beg softly. "Another, please, Sir?"

Liam smiles. "Of course, love." His mouth dips between my neck and my shoulder on the other side as his cock still works in and out of me. He starts sucking again and the euphoria is clouding my brain so much I'm seeing spots.

He's like something out of my books come to life. He feels too fucking perfect to be real. For a second my brain starts to trip out and think maybe nothing is real, maybe I've imagined it all, maybe I have truly gone insane and lost myself into one of my books. But the I promptly realize I don't fucking care because I have him and all I need is him. Putting my momentary existential crisis aside for now I force myself to focus back on the man holding me.

Liam bites me hard like he somehow knows I need to be grounded back in reality. "Focus on me." He purrs.

I shake my head a little. "How did you know?"

"Your eyes went blank and you went quiet." He mutters into my skin, still kissing at it. "Pay attention to me, Riley. You spend so much time living in your head. Don't live there, live here with me."

I nod, wanting that. "Yes." I whisper.

"You let yourself fall in love with characters and pages, you never hold onto anything real." Liam says, his voice breathy as he fucks me, "I see you, Riley, disconnected from the world, disconnected from everyone, hiding behind your laptop screen. Don't hide from me, Riley."

"I don't want to." I shake my head softly. "I don't want to hide from you, Liam."

"You couldn't even if you tried." He growled. "You're mine and even in your mind I will come fucking find you."

I nod blindly, breathing him in like he's the only oxygen I will ever need on this Earth. Feeling him against me like he's the only thing connecting me to the world.

Liam gives a few more solid thrusts into me before clamping his teeth down on my shoulder with a groan and cumming between my legs. I feel him twitch inside of me as he starts to take breaths to steady himself. After a second he lifts me off of him and sets me down.

It's a struggle not to just collapse onto the floor of the airplane bathroom, but I somehow manage to keep myself upright. Liam must realize that I'm having trouble because after tucking his cock back into his pants he grabs me and holds me upright.

I stare up at him and I can just about fucking see the words hanging in the air between us even if I can't fucking say them. I can't fucking say them. That would be insane. I can't feel this way about him. I shouldn't feel this way about him.

"I love you, Riley." Liam whispers.

The whole planes shakes with turbulence and something about it rattles my brain too seeming to knock some crazy part of me loose because despite everything, I fucking say this, "I think I love you too."

Chapter Nineteen

Liam

"What do we know about the Duboises wearabouts?" Gabriel asks me, lounged out in the chair at the head of the dining table in our new suite, which of course I booked because thirty percent of my job is fucking personal assistant. Not the point.

I click up the tracking data. "Everything. I was able to use the cars to find their house, but also and this is my recommendation, the bar they frequent, they put their cars in a garage and leave for hours. It would be easy enough to just sneak in and drive off with them."

Gabriel nods, his fingers tapping on the dark wooden table. The Eiffel Tower sits in the floor to ceiling windows behind him. The space is nice, but it doesn't have a private pool or a terrace so Riley and Gianna are beyond bored. There is however a kitchen, I can smell the melted chocolate from the brownies Riley is making in there from here. Gianna has asked for chocolate for a reason I didn't need to know about and this was Riley's way of helping.

"How do you know when the next time they will be at the bar is?" Gabriel asks.

I shrug. "That's the problem, I don't. They go often enough I can tell it's a regular place, but they don't have a set schedule. I'm just going to have to watch the tracking data and wait."

"But that only gets us one of the cars." Gabriel counters. "What's your plan for the other one?"

I shake my head. "They drive separately. Mrs. Dubois seems to like to leave early, typically with her girl friends based on security camera footage. Mr. Dubois on the other hand stays until he just about can't stand and then drives home at close. She's the limiting factor for how fast we have to be, but she's still usually in there a few hours." Keyword being usually. I've seen days where she only stayed ten minutes, but I'm trying to be an optimist. Different for me, I know.

"Sounds like we'd be doing the streets of Paris a favor by taking the cars off their hands." Gabriel mutters. "I like it. Tell me when they are at the bar again." He pushes off the table and goes over to the warm yellow gold couch. He grabs Gianna's hand. "Let's go get you a heating pad, you've been groaning for the last ten minutes."

Gianna nods and follows behind him in a very non Gianna fashion showing just how much pain she is in.

I close my laptop, leaving it on the rounded dining table and head back towards the kitchen to find Riley. The kitchen is small with a line of white cabinets and marble countertops across the back of the room. There is a counter top that juts out across the space with two barstools behind it.

The floors are made of an orange and white checkered tile and the heat of the oven is warming the room. There are windows behind the counter that look out onto the street with the light coming in to flood Riley's form.

Her back is to the door as she tosses in a cup of flour. Riley's honey blonde hair is up in a messy bun, likely to keep it out of the food. My t-shirt hangs loose on her body with her black ripped leggings underneath it. Her glasses are falling down her face, as she leans into her shoulder to push them up she sees me in the door and smiles. Fucking smiles.

"Hi." Riley says softly, her attention being dragged away from what she was doing and now going fully to me.

I come up behind her wrapping myself around her backside. "Hi, love." I purr in her ear. "How's making brownies going?"

She bristles a little. "They don't have what I usually use here," She shrugs, "But I made do with the groceries we got."

I start kissing at the marks I left previously on her neck. "Out of your books for a little while?" I ask her, pressing my lips to her neck.

"For now." She tells me. "Gianna needs these." She mixes the brownies with a whisk, her arm working slightly with the thicker batter now that there's flour in it. "I need to get back though when I'm done with this. Someone distracted me on the plane yesterday and I got nothing done."

I chuckle. "I think you got *some* things accomplished." I counter, biting down on her hickey.

The sun is starting to set out the window behind her and it's lighting her skin in golden tones that's one of the most beautiful things I've ever seen.

Her engagement ring sits heavy in my pocket as I try for the life of me to remind myself that there's so many better ways I could propose than in some random hotel kitchen. But if that's true then why is my hand itching to reach into my pocket?

"Riley?" I whisper.

She turns her head up to look at me. "Yeah?" She asks softly.

My heart races and for a brief second, I almost think better of it. I almost stop myself short and don't do it. I see myself just telling her that she's beautiful, having some peaceful chit chat, and letting her make the brownies. But I've always been one to take a risk.

I spin her around so she's facing me and drop down on one knee, a part of me sure she's going to fucking say no because why the hell should she say yes? But I pull the ring box out of my pocket and by that point it's too late to change course.

Fuck it.

"Riley, will you marry me?"

She stares at me and I see the million things she's thinking behind her eyes even if I can't hear them. I've been spilling blood with my stomach cut open and inches away from dying and somehow this is fucking scarier than that was. That was oddly peaceful... not the point.

The moment seems to stretch on for eternity before she finally mutters. "I'm fucking insane...You're fucking insane." Riley chews on her lip. "Why am I even considering this?"

"Because you love me... you think." I smirk, not really feeling it. I know I told her she was marrying me regardless of what she wanted, but honestly... I want her to *want* to marry me. I want her to want us to be together.

"I should say no." She brushes some of her hair out of her eyes.

"But you haven't." I say optimistically.

Riley shakes her head. "No, I haven't." Her eyes look away for a brief second like she's ashamed. "I don't think I could say *no* if I tried."

"So?" I question. "Is that a yes?"

Riley nods softly. "Yes." She whispers.

I take her hand and she lets me. I slide the ring on to her finger and Riley looks down at it. The white gold ring is a four carat diamond emerald cut with a split setting that is lined with little diamonds all on the side. It's elegant and proves that it's expensive without being gaudy.

"Fucking hell..." Riley mutters. "Are we engaged right now?"

I nod. "Yeah, I do think that's what just happened." I chuckle, running my thumb over the ring I just put on her finger.

Riley nods back. "Then you should probably kiss me before I think better of this because at some point I'm going to snap to my senses."

I push to my feet. "Snap to your senses later." I pull her into me and press my lips against hers. She kisses me back in a rough push and pull that has both of us panting to catch our breath. I push the mixing bowl and anything else on the counter to the side before lifting Riley up onto it.

Riley throws her arms around my neck leaning into me and wrapping her legs around my torso. "This is fucking insane." She mutters, leaning back in to kiss me as her legs and arms pull me up against the counter closer to her.

"Then we can be insane together." I promise her.

"Yes." She hums into my lips, one of her hands drifting down my chest and to my pants. "Fuck, I need you." She rubs the outside of my jeans, her eyes alight with desire.

I smile. "Say it again." I demand softly.

"I need you, Liam." Riley repeats.

"Now tell me you love me." I kiss down her jawline, peppering kisses to her neck. "For real this time, Riley. Say it like you fucking mean it and I'll slide my cock between your legs."

"I love you." She moans out without a second thought.

"Good fucking girl." I groan. My fingers dip into her leggings and I pull them down her body leaving her half naked on the flour covered counter. I kiss further down her neck and stop when I get to the collar of the t-shirt.

Riley must not like that because she quickly reaches down and pulls the shirt up and over her head. She tosses it across the kitchen before grabbing my head and pulling it back to her body.

I resume my kisses, moving down towards her nipples before pulling one into my mouth and sucking hard. The tip starts to harden under my swirling tongue and I hear a moan slip from Riley's lips.

Out of the corner of my eye I see a knife block behind her and reach over to grab the butcher knife off the rack. Riley hears it slip free and gasps. I can feel her about to move, but I pin her down with my free hand.

"Don't struggle, love." I purr. "Wouldn't want you to get hurt." I tell her and she goes still.

Riley whimpers as I slowly drag the blunt side of the knife down her side. The blade looks beautiful glimmering against her in the lasts of the daylight.

I can tell her heart is beating out of her chest by the way her breath is catching and how wide her eyes are when I glance up at them. The fear lacing through her is palpable in the kitchen as I bring the knife across her stomach. "It's the dull side, I promise." As I drag it softly over her goosebump covered flesh.

She nods but I can tell she's just about not breathing. I can tell the only reason she's not about to run out of the kitchen is because the knife is touching her skin. She doesn't trust her fiance.

Shame.

I would fix that, but fucking with her is too much fun. I like watching her squirm. I like the look in her eyes when I see that adrenaline spike and suddenly all she can do is focus on *me*. She should focus on me.

I bring down the knife to the outside of her thigh. I rest the tip on the counter and hear it scrape against it as I slowly move the dull edge down from her hip to her knee.

"Liam." Riley whimpers, her eyes glossy as the fear makes a tear slip down her face.

I lean up and lick the tear away, tasting the salty liquid as my rough tongue runs over her cheek. "Don't cry, Riley." I bring the knife up and run it down the outside of her thigh again. "I can't think straight when your breath hitches like that. You want me thinking straight, don't you?"

She nods. "Sorry, Sir." She sniffles and tries to regain her composure against the soft threats I just made. Riley's hands ball into fists as she does her best to keep herself steady and I can tell she's digging her nails into her palms, her new ring glinting as she does.

"Can you think straight right now, Riley?" I ask her softly.

She shakes her head. "No."

"No, what?" I challenge, bringing the knife back to her side.

"No, Sir." She rushes out her breath hitching in that way that has me all kinds of fucked up. This woman is going to be the death of me.

I slide the knife back into the knife rack, deciding I've tortured her enough with it for the time being before grabbing her around the waist and pulling her off the counter.

Riley shrieks softly and then gasps when I spin her around to bend her over the counter behind us. I push her into the marble countertop and her hands try on instinct to push herself upright, but I pin her down.

"Liam." She whimpers.

I unzip my jeans, pulling my cock out and stroking it briefly to make sure I'm hard enough to go in her, I am. I'm hard as a fucking rock after seeing that knife against her skin. "Riley." I reply back to her, as I run my head over her entrance. "Fuck, you're soaked."

She shakes her head like she's trying to deny it. "I..." She mutters out like she feels she needs to justify herself for being turned on by the same fucked up shit I am.

"You don't have to explain yourself to me, Riley." I put my hand on the small of her back to keep her in place as I start to push inside of her. "We can just be depraved together."

Riley whimpers again, but I feel her trying to push against my hold to back herself further on to my cock. She fucking wants this, wants me.

"That's it, Riley." I slide myself further into her. "That's my good girl."

She moans as I seat myself fully inside of her, waiting a second for her to adjust before I start to fuck her. The second she seems like she's got her bearings I pull back out and slam into her hard. Riley lets out a scream that I'm sure Gabriel and Gianna heard from down the hall, not that they are going to come check.

I dig my hands into her hips as I fuck her, feeling her soft skin mold against my hand. I hope she has nail marks on her fucking waist for days. I'm half tempted to dig in harder just to make sure she does. So that when she goes dress shopping she'll look in the mirror and see the marks I left on her and think of me.

"Fuck." Riley cries out breathily.

I grab her and haul her torso up enough that I'm able to slip my hand over her mouth. "Shhh. Someone's going to think you're in trouble." I groan in her ear before pinching her nose shut.

Riley gasps her hands shooting up to try and wrestle mine off her nose and mouth. She is trying desperately to suck down breath and I can tell because I feel the suction on my hand, but she can't get any air. "Liam." Her muffled mutter comes through my hand.

"Feel light headed yet, love?" I ask her with a chuckle.

She thrashes, no longer caring about anything but trying to get oxygen as her body goes into fight or flight. Then I slam into her and she shrieks. Her fighting starts to slow and only then do I yank my hand off her face. Riley takes a gasping breath with a growled, "Fuck. You." coming out in between pants.

I oblige her request, pressing a hand to her back to push her back down onto the marble as I thrust into her hard. "If you insist, love." I purr.

Riley's body seems to go limp under her as breath saws in and out of her lungs mixed with gasps as I continue to drill into her. She turns her head to the side and I can see that her eyes have just about rolled back. She looks delirious with pleasure and fear and whatever other range of emotions I sent coursing through her.

"You're such a good slut for me, Riley." I groan as I give a few more hard strokes and feel myself approaching the precipice. Riley moans and I slam into her hard, filling her pussy with my cum.

"Liam." She mutters, her voice far off and tired.

I shush her softly before picking her limp body up into my arms. I start to carry her back into the bedroom so she can lay down.

"The brownies?" Riley waves a hand back towards the kitchen like she's telling me to take her back so she can finish making them for Gia.

I shake my head. "You need to go lay down. Don't worry about the brownies though." I press a kiss to her forehead. "I'll finish making them, love."

Chapter Twenty

Riley

Gabriel is scowling as we walk through the doors of the small bridal shop in the upscale part of Paris. The store has elegant curtains draped around the inside of the front door and a sign that says by appointment only. We had to be buzzed in when we got here.

"You didn't have to come, you sourpuss." Gianna huffs. "Either smile or go back to the hotel. This is a big moment for a woman and I will not have your piss poor attitude yucking up one of the biggest days of Riley's life.

The place is like shopping in a fluffy white cloud. There's so many dresses around I couldn't even count them all if I tried. Plush blue couches covered in pillows sit in the back of the space surrounding a small platform that's in front of a mirror. There's a blue curtained off area to the left of that and doors off to the right.

"I still don't trust her out alone and Liam couldn't fucking come with because of your stupid insistance on that old superstition so I had no choice." Gabriel grumbles.

The older blonde sales woman leads us back towards the couches gesturing for us all to take a seat. "Bonjour, I'm Aimee and I will be helping you today. Which one of you is Riley?" She asks, looking between me and Gianna.

I take a deep breath trying to steady myself and not think too much about what is happening right now. I had *asked* Liam for the anxiety medication this morning, but he insisted that I would be better off with alcohol instead and proceeded to pour me a shot of whiskey. I downed it, and then the second one he poured before Gianna pulled me out the door asking if I was wearing appropriate underwear for dress shopping. I had no idea what that meant, still don't, but Gianna did make me change and put on nipple pasties before we left.

"I'm Riley." I say on an exhale probably not quite seeming like the blushing brides she's used to. I collapse down onto one of the couches and Gabriel and Gianna sit down on a different one.

Aimee smiles. "Wonderful!" She grabs my hand apparently not letting me sit down and drags me up onto the small podium in the center of the room. "And when is the wedding?"

I look to Gianna and Gabriel, having no idea the answer to that question. I thoroughly have no control over any of this and apparently I'm starting to become okay with that since I was delusional enough to actually say yes when Liam proposed to me. Why the fuck did I say yes? Why haven't I tried to give him the ring back?

I should have thrown the damned thing off my finger the second Liam pulled the knife from the butcher block. Fuck, I shouldn't have let him put it on in the first place. But then I glance down at the shimmering rock at my finger and suddenly every thought vanishes from my head but Liam.

"June twenty second." Gianna smiles.

My stomach sinks thinking about how close that is. Is it rude if I ask for champagne? Gianna told me this place had champagne and I definitely need alcohol right now. Those two shots of whiskey were not nearly enough.

"Ah, June weddings are so lovely." Aimee hums, raising my arms and starting to measure me. "Who picked the date, you or hubby to be?"

"He did." I answer softly, trying not to shake as she wraps the tape around my bust.

Aimee loosens the tape dropping down to around my hips. "He has good taste then, huh? Both in women and wedding dates."

I just nod.

She measures a few other things before moving over to the small table on the side and writing some things down. "I'll be right back with some of the things we have either in your size or close enough to get altered. It's too close to the date to order, but we have plenty of options." Then she walks off into the many rows of dresses.

"Try not to look like you're miserable." Gabriel mutters.

I glare at him.

"We need drinks and food!" Gianna says cheerfully, ignoring her husband. She runs after Aimee into the stacks of dresses, her heels clicking on the tile floor as she does.

I sigh and adjust my crop top feeling very out of place in somewhere this high end. I'm a little surprised they let me in dressed like this. Gianna told me on the car ride over that after we get my wedding dress we are going out shopping because she, in her words, *can't keep being seen with someone who's dressed like they make their own clothes from shit they buy at the thrift store.* I wanted to argue with her, but I did get this blue tie dye tee at a thrift store and then cut it down to a crop top and removed the collar... I don't know how she knew.

"She didn't ask me for my budget." I whisper to Gabriel.

He scoffs. "Did Liam give you a budget when he handed you his black card?" He asks and I shake my head. "Yeah, that's because the people who shop at places like this don't have *budgets* and neither do you now, Riley."

"There's gonna be a lot of zeros on the price tag of this dress, aren't there?" I say more to myself than him.

"If I were you, I just wouldn't look." Gabriel chuckles. "That's Liam's problem, not yours. And he can always settle up with me later if he needs the help." I get a little worried at that and Gabriel must see it cause he waves me off. "He won't. I promise. Liam is very good at what he does and because of that I compensate him well for it. His bank account could probably handle three of these dresses before he even broke a sweat."

I shake my head. "None of this is making me feel better."

Gianna comes rushing back through the rows. "Aimee's assistant will be back in a minute with the cake and champagne. You clearly need a drink with a face like that."

I grimace which probably doesn't help my case. "Remind me again, why are we friends?"

"Because I teach you the Italian curse words you need to cuss out your fiance." Gianna smiles, going to sit back down next to Gabriel.

I roll my eyes, but Gianna can tell I'm joking. She's fun and I feel a lot less crazy for liking to have her around than for liking to have Liam around. Honestly even Gabriel is growing on me.

"Bonjour." A younger blonde woman greets, holding a bottle of champagne and three glasses. "I'm Sophie. I'll be assisting Aimee today." Sophie and Aimee look almost exactly alike except that Sophie is about twenty years younger leading me to believe this is a family business. "I'll be back with snacks in a moment." She says, setting the bottle down on the side table beside Gianna before going back through the door off to the side.

Gianna doesn't wait for Sophie to come back before grabbing the champagne bottle and popping it open, somehow managing not to let the cork go flying as she does so. She pours three glasses, passing me the first one. "To the bride to be!"

"I'll chug to that." I mutter, downing the entire glass in one go.

Gianna laughs. "Too late to go back now, you already accepted the ring. That means you're stuck with us for life now." She takes a sip of her own glass. "We should go get some of that matching permanent jewelry." She suggests. "Matching bracelets would be so cute!"

"Why do I not hate that idea?" I step down off my podium and move over to the bottle, pouring myself a second glass.

"Because I'm your ride or die and you finally love me back." Gia raises her glass and I find myself raising mine back.

"Knowing you, the answer is gonna be die." I chuckle.

Gianna shrugs. "That was one of the op-tions."

Gabriel sighs, starting to play on his phone and pretending he's not paying attention even though knowing him, he probably is.

Aimee comes back with dresses, hanging them up on a rack near the curtain before waving me over to her. "Come, let's try some things on. I picked you a little bit of every-thing so we can see what is most you and then choose something more specific from there."

I follow blindly into the curtained off area as Sophie sets down what can only be described as a cake charcuterie board and comes behind me to close the curtain.

Awkwardly, consider there's two random women in the room I don't fucking know, I take off my shirt and leggings. Aimee has me step into one of the dresses, but I can't really tell anything about it as it's currently just a puddle of fabric on the floor. She pulls it up around me and uses some fabric clamps off a table beside me to secure the dress. I look down at the white dress with the beads and the silk and the fucking engagement ring, that is really fucking heavy by the way, and try not to have a panic attack.

Aimee ushers me out from behind the curtain bringing me over to stand on the podium and fluffing the dress behind me so it billows out with the flowing gown. The a line dress has thick straps to support the heavy top with beads and lace covering the bust that dissolves into silk all the way down to the ground. The train is long and has lace coming up from the back of it covering the tail but not the skirt. Buttons go all the way down from where the dress ends low on my back to the end of the train.

And as I'm staring at myself, my blonde hair flowing around this beautiful dress, I catch sight of the hickeys in the mirror. I didn't even know this man at the beginning of the month and now he's got me trying on fucking wedding dresses with his bite marks imprinted on my skin like a brand.

"Holy shit." I mutter.

"Beautiful." Gianna smiles, her mouth full of cake. She starts to wash it down with more champagne as she slugs Gabriel on the shoulder.

"Yes, very pretty." He says dryly, glancing up from his phone. When Gianna looks at him annoyed he mouths, *What?* But I'm not really paying that much attention to their interaction because all I can pay attention to is the ten pound dress weighing me down to hell.

I gasp, my body shaking and Gianna gets up off the couch to come hold my hand. "Gianna, what am I fucking doing?" I look at her and she pulls me into a hug.

"Riley." She whispers, rubbing my back around the clamps holding together the dress. After a minute when I'm no longer shaking and stop feeling like I'm going to cry Gianna pulls away. She snatches the glass out of Gabriel's hand and he grumbles but she just passes it to me. "You need this more than he does."

I kick it back quickly, sure that Aimee and Sophie must think I'm insane for the way I'm acting. I turn back to the mirror and see that I didn't actually avoid crying like I thought I did. "Sorry." I apologize.

Aimee waves me off. "All women handle wedding jitters differently. I had one girl shred one of my dresses with her bare hands. Given she had sharp nails." She laughs softly.

I chuckle back. "No dresses will be harmed, I promise."

Aimee just shrugs. "As I look at it, I sold two dresses that day. Who am I to decide if you wear them or not?"

I lose myself for a second in the thought of a woman ripping a dress apart before turning back to the mirror. "This doesn't feel like me." I say softly.

Gianna smiles. "Then we'll find one that does."

Aimee, Sophie, and Gianna have squeezed me into no less than thirty dresses by this point. I was keeping count at first but then I lost track. I've been a white cloud for the last two or three or five hours... time is irrelevant now. None of the dresses have felt right and I'm starting to think that's because *this* isn't right. I'm about ready to throw the damned engagement ring at the wall and run from the place screaming. The only reason I haven't is because I don't want to learn if Gabriel's threat to kill me if I caused problems was real.

"None of them have that..." Gianna waves her hand in the air like she's trying to grasp for words, "Je ne sais quoi." She sighs. "Do you have something different from the ones we've been trying? Something with less tulle and fluffy. I just don't think the extravagant is very her."

Most of the dresses they've stuffed me into are very princess gowns in different fonts and none of that really has hit right. All of them have had long trains and fluffed skirts and loads of lace and beads. It's honestly been so overwhelming that I've just been staring at most of them and not saying anything. Gianna and Aimee however have had *lengthy* conversations about the problems with each dress and keep trying to find ones that fix those issues.

Aimee disappears into the rows of dresses again seeming to have an extra sense of determination this time. Sophie has brought out another plate full of different snacks because of how long we have been here.

"Gianna." I step off the podium in the extra fluffy dress I have on right now, knowing I'm about to be corralled into the curtain again to go change. "This is hopeless. I don't even know if I want this and none of what has happened today with any of these dresses have helped that feeling. You guys keep saying when it's the right dress I'll know. Maybe there's a reason none of these are right."

She looks at me sadly, rubbing my lace covered arm gently. "Riley, it's just a dress. This is not some big metaphor even if I'm sure you want to make it one. It's a piece of fabric that you're going to wear twice, once when you walk down the aisle and the second time when your marriage is falling apart for the first time and you're trying to bring the spark back to life."

I huff a laugh and glance over to see Gabriel scowling. "You didn't need to tell her that." He mutters.

Gianna just ignores him. "It's just a dress." She repeats. "Don't overthink it. At the end of that day, what you're wearing will be the furthest thing from your mind."

And that somehow feels very very true. The dress definitely will not be my biggest problem on my wedding day. Maybe I should be more concerned with those bigger problems, but for some reason I do relax a little, because Gia's right, this is just picking a dress.

Aimee comes running back through the stacks holding a much smaller looking gown than all the others I've tried on. There's no lace, no beads, no big fluffy princess skirt, no mile long train. "This one. This is it. I know it is." She grabs my hand and yanks me back towards the curtain.

I shimmy out of the current dress before passing it to Sophie. Aimee has me take my bra back off for this one since it is an off the shoulder dress. After the first two or three I became a lot less self conscious about being naked in front of these women.

Aimee zips me into the soft fabric and when I glance back over my shoulder she's smiling. "It's the perfect size. All you'd need to have altered is the hem." She shakes her head like she's in awe as she stares at me, but I have no idea what she's looking at because there's no mirror in here. She rushes me back out the curtain and the second I catch sight of myself, I freeze.

The dress is a mermaid gown that starts billowing out midway on my thigh. It's soft and silky with flowing fabric that seems to float around me, none of it laying stiff or rigid. The train is small, enough that it flutters but not so much that it's dragging behind me. It sits off my shoulder with the ivory fabric draping around in elegant folds like it was softly wrapped around me with one side laid over the other leaving a slight v in the neck-line.

I don't even finish walking to the podium. I just get stuck on the edge of the space staring at myself, trying to come to grips with that I've never felt so beautiful and so much like myself in something I've worn.

Gianna smiles as she looks at me. "Bellissima."

I nod as Aimee finally pulls me up onto the podium to look at myself fully in the mirror.

"You're missing something." Sophie beams, running off to the wall of veils on the side and pulling a shorter one with diamonds rimmed around the outside free from the rack. She comes over to me and buries the clip in my hair before adjusting it around me. "Beautiful."

Gianna sniffles. "Oh, Riley." She wipes at her eyes with the back of her hand. "You bitch, you're gonna make me wreck my mascara."

I chuckle at her joke finally being pulled from my stupor. "Holy shit... It's... It's perfect." I turn to Aimee. "I... I think I love it." And I laugh remembering saying the same thing to Liam.

"Not bad for a day's work if I do say so my-self." Aimee dusts her hands. "Your fiance will be very pleased."

"Yeah..." I mutter. "I think he will be."

Chapter Twenty One

Liam

I hear the alert go off on my phone when my head is between Riley's legs and have a hard time in that moment trying to remember exactly *why* I like my job. I pull away before she gets a chance to finish on my tongue and she whimpers as my head leaves her. "Fucking hell." I mutter going to grab my phone off the nightstand in the hotel bedroom.

The Duboises just arrived at the bar and because I have no idea how long Mrs. Dubois is going to be there, we have to go *now*. Gabriel and I have been waiting over a week for them to go back to this bar and we can't let the opportunity slide.

"I'm sorry, love." I push away from the white bedding and start to rummage through my suitcase for a black button up. "I gotta go."

Riley bristles. "What the hell?" She stares at me with wide eyes, completely naked except for the glasses that are sliding down her face. "Are you mad at me?"

I tug on a pair of pants and the button up, trying to get dressed as fast as physically possible but stop when she says that. "No, Riley." I walk over to her and press a kiss to her forehead, my lips still wet from licking her, leaving a print on her skin. "It's a work thing. It can't wait. I'm so sorry."

She lets out a shuddering breath like she's trying to calm herself and nods softly. "Okay." She whispers. "Work is work. I get it. I guess." She shrugs but it feels very half hearted.

"I'll make this up to you." I brush her hair away from her face and kiss her softly. "I promise." I want to comfort her longer, but I have to go.

I rush out of the room and see Gabriel sitting at the dining table. "The Duboises are at the bar." I tell him, grabbing my gun off the table and tucking it into the back of my pants before adjusting my shirt to cover it. I slip a knife into my boot as well, just for good measure.

Gabriel is almost always work ready and I rarely see him wear anything else. He doesn't have to grab his gun, already having it on him, before nodding to the door and starting to head out. "When did you get the alert?" He asks, leading me towards the elevators.

"Just a minute ago." I respond. "I got dressed the second it went off."

Gabriel scoffs. "Considering the noises coming from your room, I'm guessing Riley wasn't too pleased by that." He chuckles as we get into the elevator and he hits the button for the ground floor.

"She's pissed." I could see it in her eyes, even though she said it was okay, it wasn't. Riley looked like she wanted to murder me, I have no doubt she's probably in there right now finishing the job I started and cursing my name as she does so.

"Buy her a tennis bracelet." Gabriel shrugs. "Always works on Gianna when I fuck up."

I roll my eyes as we head off the elevator and exit the hotel into the street. "I'll keep that in mind."

"You could have just said, *no*." Gabriel chuckles.

The bar isn't particularly close, but we have to walk though because we both need to be able to drive the cars back out. I tried to pick a hotel closer to the bar but finding one nice enough on such short notice was hard enough as it was. It's about a three block walk which is doable enough given not fun when you're somewhere as crowded as Paris.

The streets are full of small buildings. Everything is close together and I constantly feel like I'm about to get trampled by a tourist. I catch sight of a French man bumping into a young woman and slipping her wallet into his pocket. This is the biggest pickpocket city in the world, it's about half the reason why I've been insistent on that Gianna and Riley can't go shopping alone. Gabriel has more than backed me up on that.

I spend most of our walk fucking with the bar and parking lot cameras on my phone trying to see if I can find where the Dubois are now. They are an older couple in their fifties, both have been in France their whole lives.

Colette keeps up with herself. Her hair highlighted blonde consistently, so much botox that she could have probably used that money to buy a moderate size house, and she spends any other money she can get from her husband on the trendiest clothing.

Antoine on the other hand seems to care more about gambling away all his money as opposed to appearances. All of the pictures I've seen of him have a worn expression across his face and his gray hair is starting to thin, likely due to stress.

I find them on the bar cameras and see the couple have already parted ways. Antoine is chatting up some younger women like his wife isn't just on the other side of the bar and Colette has found some friends to hang around.

"We need to hurry." I tell Gabriel as we get closer. Colette hanging out with her friends very well could turn into them going somewhere else. She may not stay more than a few minutes.

What does help our cause is that the sun is starting to set. The darkness will help keep our actions more covert and the fact that it's on the cusp mean the streetlights might not go up until we've already made our move.

We get to the parking garage and I still haven't been able to find the cars on the cameras. The tracking helps but there's a few floors and we have no way of knowing which one they are on.

Gabriel and I split up checking the different floors. After a few minutes I get a call from him. "Hers is on three, his is on four." Gabriel says by way of greeting. "If you can unlock his remotely I'm by it now."

"Give me a second." I tell him, pulling the phone away from my ear. These cars are high end enough that they have remotes that you can connect to your phone. It's needless in my opinion and not even slightly secure. Besides why can't you just use keys like everyone fucking else? But what rich jackasses choose to do with their money isn't really my problem.

I open up the app that I have synced to their cars and unlock Antoine's car. I hit the remote start and that should be enough for Gabriel to be able to get in and drive it off. These things are stupid expensive and with that comes stupid features so they don't require the keys if you have the pin that I entered into the app.

"Should be good." I tell Gabriel.

"If this car alarm goes off, Riley's not going to get a chance to kill you." Gabriel says gruffly through the phone. After a second and the sound of a car door opening and closing on the other side of the line with no sirens I assume I get to keep my life for tonight. Although the night is still early and I don't know what Riley plans for me when I get back.

"I'm heading to three now." I tell him, walking over to the elevator in the parking garage.

"I'll see you at the meeting spot." Gabriel responds before hanging up the phone.

The elevator doors open and I take it down to three. I get there and start to head to where the tracker shows the car is on the floor, but then I hear voices coming from by the car.

I duck in between two other cars as I see blonde hair flying in the small breeze that's coming in. I peek out from between the cars and see Colette and a bunch of the women who were in the bar gathered around her car.

"Shit."

We weren't fast enough.

I grab my phone and dial Gabriel again. He picks up on the first ring. "Have you left yet?" I ask him.

"No." Gabriel says. "I'm about to come down."

I sneak away from the women and start heading towards the fourth floor, at a full out sprint once I'm far enough away. "Colette went back to the car already."

Gabriel grumbles through the phone. "Fuck."

"She's with a bunch of other women." I tell him. "They are probably heading to another bar. We could tail them and try to grab the car there."

"Yeah." He sighs. "It's our best option. Once Antoine realizes his car is gone, they are going to be on high alert and it's going to be a lot harder to get hers. We need to try and grab it tonight."

"Agreed." I see the black sports car Gabriel is in and pull open the passenger door. "The car has a tracker, we don't have to follow close."

He groans. "Why can't it ever just be easy?"

"Corbin and Monreaux went down easy enough." I shrug. "Gotta have at least a little challenge. What fun is life without it?"

Gabriel rolls his eyes. "Is that why you decided to acquire a wife by kidnapping her?"

"What can I say?" I smirk. "I like a little struggle." And as if Riley could fucking hear me, the tracker on her ankle alerts on my phone. "Speaking of which."

"Riley?" Gabriel asks.

I nod. "Yup. Apparently she was more than a little mad about the orgasm I forgot since she decided to skip out on me."

Gabriel picks up his phone from the cup holder and calls Gianna. "Are you with Riley?" He growls into the phone. "You are both in so much trouble when we get back." The face he makes is fucking feral and I know Gianna must be taunting the bull. "I'm going to make you pay for that."

"Can you tell her to say the same thing to Riley?" I mutter. "She's in so much trouble."

"Hold on." Gabriel says gruffly, hitting the speakerphone button.

"Gianna and I decided since you both *abandoned* us," Riley says, stressing the word so hard I huff a laugh, "That we would just have to make our own fun. What did you expect us to do? Sit in that boring ass hotel room all night?"

"Riley, if you don't turn back around right the fuck now, I'm going to-" I had any number of colorful threats in mind but she interrupts me.

"We'll be back before midnight." I can hear the smirk in her voice.

"Two a.m.!" Gianna corrects and then the phone call ends.

I'm left scowling as we follow Colette's car out of the parking garage. Every part of me wants to go after her right this damned second, but I know that's not an option. Gianna will keep her safe. She has the tracker. She *said* she was coming back. But this is the first time I've truly had to loosen up the reigns and it's fucking terrifying.

"Turn at the next street." I just about growl through my gritted teeth.

"You're overreacting." And the fact that Gabriel is the one fucking telling me that is really saying something.

"Thank you for your input." I huff out. "Left here." I point as we follow about two cars behind Colette and her friends.

Gabriel laughs. "I have no fucking idea how you didn't get caught cheating at baccarat when you wear your thoughts on your face like that."

"That was work." I keep my eyes on the tracking data for Colette and have to fight not to check Riley's. "It's different when it comes to her."

"She's with Gia." Gabriel says. "Gia might be willing to let her run around Paris, but she's not going to let her run around on her own. She won't let Riley slip off."

I nod. "I know that. I just... I don't like her having the opportunity."

"She's not going to take it." Gabriel tells me, sounding way more confident in that than I am.

I shake my head. "How are you so sure?"

"Because she hadn't tried to up until now." Gabriel says. "Next right?" He asks and I nod. "If Riley was going to run she would have when we were taking her to the airport in Italy, or when we were in Monaco, or any fucking time before now when we took her out in public. She's had *plenty* of opportunities. And I'm not going to pretend to understand *why* but she's staying for some reason. Your research on Stockholm syndrome must have paid off." He chuckles.

I huff a laugh. "Yeah, I guess."

"She likes you." Gabriel says, since apparently I still didn't seem convinced. He's right though, I'm not. I still think she's going to try and run. "She likes you enough that she let you put a ring on her finger after knowing you for like two weeks even with the fact that you kidnapped her. So loosen the leash a little. If she starts to pull you can always tighten it again."

"A leash might not be a half bad idea after tonight." I mutter.

Gabriel glares at me briefly. "You're missing the point." He says following Colette into a new parking garage.

"I get the point." I tell him. "There's a parking spot here. Don't get any closer, we can't have her recognizing the car."

Gabriel rolls his eyes. "Thank you, captain obvious, I wouldn't have known any of those things without your help."

"You're welcome." I mutter, getting out of the car the second he parks it. "Wait two minutes and if I don't call you, I'll see you at the meeting spot."

Gabriel nods as I close the door and head deeper into the parking garage.

I start flicking at my phone trying to get the car to unlock but it's not working. I don't know what the fuck it's doing, nor do I have time to figure it out, but the remote is popping back an error.

Colette and her friend go to get on the elevator and I quickly adlib a new plan as I chase after them waving a hand.

Once again, French, moving on.

"Pardon me, ladies, please hold the elevator!" I shout politely, running up to get on.

The women all blush softly, and thank god one of them actually does press the elevator hold button. She waits for me to get on before letting go of the button.

"Thank you." I smile, not bothering to hit a button since they already pushed the one for street level.

Colette slips her keys into her pocket and turns to one of her friends, whispering something in her ear that I don't manage to catch with how softly she spoke.

The friend giggles and I hear something to the effect of, "If you're gonna cheat on your husband with anyone it should be a hot stranger, lord knows he's done it to you enough times."

Colette hushes her, but I turn around.

"Can I help you ladies?" I purr softly.

Colette's eyes go wide. "No, sorry. She's just being stupid. Too much to drink." The second the elevator opens Colette goes to rush out and in her haste it's easy enough for me to "accidentally" bump into her.

"Oh, pardon me." I apologize as I pull the keys out of her jacket pocket and quickly slip my hands back into my slacks.

She smiles softly. "You're fine." Colette grabs one of her friend's hand and just about runs away. I can hear her cursing her friend out telling her how embarrassed she was.

I pretend to walk a little bit the other way for a solid minute and when I check over my shoulder they are gone. I make my way back to the elevator and down through the parking garage again. From there driving off with the car was easy enough.

I reach the meeting spot where Gabriel and I are going to hide the cars until morning shortly after and he's already waiting for me. Tomorrow we will leave to take them back to Venice for our Italian friends but tonight, I have a different problem I have to go deal with.

Riley.

Chapter Twenty Two

Riley

I chuckle as Gianna passes me another shot.

"Salute!" She cheers, clinking her glass against mine. "Those fuckers will regret ditching us! We know how to have fun on our own."

I kick back the shot without a second thought, not knowing what it was because I didn't pay that much attention when Gianna ordered. I was too busy sulking, not able to get my mind off Liam just vanishing seconds after pulling his lips off my clit. Bastard. Stronzo. "I need another." I growl.

Gia chuckles. "Let's move to real drinks." She says waving back over the bartender.

The bar she found was smaller and seems to be filled with more locals than tourists.

The black and white checkerboard flooring is a little sticky against my heeled boots. There are black couches and chairs with tables surrounding them rather than just regular tables or booths. The walls are a burgundy red lit up by the glass chandeliers hanging throughout the space.

We are sitting at the black bar stools. The dark wooden bar stretches across the space rounding close to the front door. There's countless bottles of alcohol behind it and as always Gia picked the most expensive ones.

"Can we do two glasses of your sweetest and most expensive red?" She purrs to the bartender, looking at him like he's currently her favorite person in the world. I'm almost offended it's not me.

The man nods and pulls out a nice bottle, pouring us two glasses and passing them across the bartop.

"Thank you." I quickly take a long sip of mine like I didn't probably just down one hundred dollars worth of wine in one go. I don't think I want to know the price of this.

Gianna made me leave my valuables at the hotel because of how common pickpockets are in this city. We each brought our cards in our bra, but our rings and everything else we left behind.

Somehow I think if Liam shows up before we leave, that may be what he's most upset about. He doesn't like when I'm not wearing my ring. At one point he pinned my wrists above my head half way through us having sex and noticed that I didn't have it on, it had been the middle of the night, of course I didn't have it on. But regardless he stopped and forced me to go get it out of the ring box before he would fuck me again.

Psycho... why do I love that?

"You seem pissed." Gianna chuckles.

I nod. "I am."

"I can tell." She takes a sip of her wine. "Especially since for once, sneaking out was your idea. What did the dumbass do?"

"He had work." I growl, gripping my glass so hard I'm surprised I didn't break it.

Gianna shrugs. "So?"

"He was already in the middle of something." I bristle, putting my fingers in a v up to my lips and licking briefly between them before creasing my face with annoyance.

Gia bursts out laughing. "He must not have finished that something." She says, her head kicking back from how hard she's fucking cackling.

"Nope." I grit out. "Fucker." She keeps giggling, but I'm already irritable as all hell. "I'm glad you think my misfortune is so hilarious." I grumble.

She waves me off, but doesn't stop. "I just think it's funny the kinds of problems newly engaged couples have. To be young and in love." She swoons.

"Aren't you, Gabriel, and Liam all the same age?" I question, more just to kick back against her statement, I already know the answer.

"Technically Liam is the oldest." Gianna says. "But regardless, I understand why you're mad. I would be punishing Gabriel if he did that to me too. Maybe we should go punish Liam's black card next." She suggests. "I know a few higher end places we haven't been to yet that are open late. There's this cute little boutique-"

She's cut off when an older man saddles up beside the bar next to us. "Bonjour, mon cheri." The man interrupts resting his hand on the back of my chair and getting way too close to me.

I try to look bored rather than pissed off because I've found that's the safest way to defend against annoying men in bars. "We were in the middle of a discussion." I say, trying to be as polite as possible.

"We are in the middle of a new one now, no?" He asks, sitting down beside me.

Gianna scoffs. "We are both married."

The man shrugs. "So am I." He smirks and the expression makes me nauseated. He's wearing a nice enough button up and slacks, but his thinning gray hair looks like he didn't even comb it. There's nothing that is attractive about this man to me and the fact that he has the audacity to try and hit on someone who's at least twenty years younger than him is disgusting.

"That makes it worse." I mutter, taking a sip of my drink.

"She's too nice to say it, but I'm not." Gianna smiles and the expression looks lethal. "Fuck off."

The man holds his hands up defensively. "My apologies, mademoiselles." He says, slinking off to one of the tables in the corner with a group of other older men.

"French men are so rude." Gianna huffs. "And never as hot as they think they are. Even the hot ones aren't as hot as they think they are."

I chuckle and take another sip of my wine. "What were we talking about before?"

Gia thinks about it for a second, tapping her fingers rhythmically on the bar as she tries to remember. "Oh! How Liam left you wanting and that we should go spend all his money."

I roll my eyes. "I don't think spending all his money will fix my problem." I kick back the rest of my glass and start to wave the bartender down again. "Besides I think *all* his money would be hard to spend in one night."

Gianna laughs. "We can start buying houses and yachts and jets. That's how you get your husband pissed fast... Not speaking from personal experience." She mutters the last part into her glass.

The bartender pours me a new glass, but Gia is still nursing hers. I'm drinking to forget, she's drinking for leisure, very different sports. "And another shot of whatever that was before, please." I ask and he obliges.

"Let's not get you too fucked up." Gianna says. "If I get you rip roaring drunk and take you out through the streets of Paris I think Liam might kill me."

I wave her off. "He'll be fine." I grumble, kicking back the new shot. "Maybe this will teach him to finish what he starts." The rush of the alcohol is starting to hit me and I'm feeling a little less like I want to punch my *fiance* in the face the next time I see him. Although, I am still considering it.

"A good lesson for him to learn." Gia nods.

I push off the barstool. "I'm going to run to the bathroom." Gianna gives me a concerned look. "I'm not going to bolt, I promise." And for whatever reason, I mean it. "I'll come back.

"You better. If you don't, I'm going to be in so much trouble." She says into her glass.

I'm about to walk away but I'm genuinely curious so I ask, "Why are you letting me do this?"

"Should I not be?" She counters.

"That's not what I meant." I shake my head.

Gia shrugs. "Riley, I see the way you look at Liam. If you run it's because you're scared, not because you don't want to be with him. Even if he went about it in the weirdest way, whatever this seems to be that's building between the

two of you is real and that's obvious to every‐
one."

"But if you do run." She sighs and gives me a soft smile. "I wouldn't even blame you and honestly, I think you should get to make the choice for yourself if you stay with him or not."

"Thanks, Gia." I say softly.

She nods. "Just come back. I'm not trying to get murdered tonight."

"I will." I promise her.

I head off to the bathrooms in the back of the bar. The women's room has a soft floral scent lacing through it. It's empty except for me but rather small with the walls tight between stalls and not much room between sinks.

I know I should run. I know this is the best chance I'm going to get, possibly ever. I could take off right now, find a way to break off this anklet and disappear into the wind. I could set up and write books anywhere. I could go to another city and blend in, spend the rest of my life hiding from Liam or at least until he gets bored... but... I don't want to do that.

Maybe it took this ounce of freedom to final‐ ly start to be okay with it, but I love Liam. And given the chance to run or to stay? For some stupid reason, I pick stay.

Marrying him is probably a mistake. Staying is probably a mistake. But it's one I think I'm okay with making. One that I can live with. Sometimes mistakes are a good thing. Planning everything makes life so rigid. Always following the book is boring. I want excitement and I think with Liam I will always have that.

My spiralling thoughts were going to continue but then my mind starts to cloud. Everything feels hazy in a way that I immediately recognize after the past few weeks with Liam.

Someone drugged me.

I finish using the bathroom quickly. I need to find Gianna. I don't know who slipped something into my drink, but I definitely know the feeling by now. It's happened to me too many times.

My mind flashes to my mother's ex boyfriend and fear spikes through my body. This is fucking bad. I stumble out of the bathroom about to b line back to Gianna when someone grabs me, covering my mouth as they pull me out a side door by the bathrooms. I go to scream and fight, but I feel tired, weak.

It's not Liam, I know that. This person is much smaller, given they are still bigger than me though. A part of me was hoping that this was my fiance trying to get back at me but it seems I wasn't that lucky.

The man pulls me out the door and slams me against the wall hard. I catch sight of the same older man who was bugging me and Gianna earlier. His breath smells more like booze this up close than I had noticed before. He holds me against the wall. "Bonjour, mon cheri."

Chapter Twenty Three

Liam

Out of all the fucking bars in all of fucking Paris Riley and Gianna for some fucking reason stumbled into the one I've been staking out for the past fucking week. Fucking hell. Can you tell how fucking pissed I am?

I have no idea what the absolute fuck Riley was thinking. She should have just stayed in the room and waited for me to come back. I promised I would make it up to her. The fact that she was so pissed that she snuck out with Gia to go drinking?

Gabriel and I storm into the bar, probably looking akin to bulls in a damned china shop. We spot Gia instantly but no Riley and my stomach drops.

"Where the hell is my fiance?" I hiss at Gia.

"Bathroom." She says quickly.

I don't wait to see what Gabriel's plans for Gia are before going over to the bathroom and pushing open the door, probably seconds away from getting myself kicked out of this bar. "RI-LEY!" I scream into the bathroom.

I wait a second and there is no response. "RILEY!" I call again. When no one says anything again I go into the bathroom. I kick open every stall and my worst fears are confirmed.

She's not here.

Growling like a fucking animal, I slam my fist into the wall so hard I split open one of my knuckles. I prowl back out of the bathroom towards Gia and she looks terrified.

Gabriel stands between me and his wife, blocking me from fucking strangling her, which I am legitimately considering in this moment. "Calm down."

I'm so fucking pissed that I almost forget to check the tracking data again. "She's not fucking in the bathroom, Gia." I say through gritted teeth. The tracking data still says she's close by, but it's not accurate enough for me to know where. What if she slipped the tracker somehow?

"I'm sorry!" Gia cried out, shrinking behind Gabriel. "I thought she would stay." Tears slide down her face. "She said she would come back."

A scoff huffed its way out of my mouth. "And you believed her?" I challenge. "You let my fiance run off by herself and just *hoped* she would come back?"

Gia shakes her head softly. "She's only been gone a couple minutes, she couldn't have gotten far." Gianna promises.

I turn on the ping I have on her tracker hoping I will be able to hear the beeping or maybe it will tell her that I'm on to her and she'll come back.

"Have you been watching the front?" Gabriel asks Gianna.

She nods. "If she left it wasn't out the front door."

I turn and head back towards the bathrooms remembering seeing an exit back there. Rage courses through my veins and I want to destroy something. I will tear this world to fucking shreds to get Riley back.

If she thinks she can get away from me she's fucking wrong. I will search every corner of the Earth until she's back in my arms again.

There's nowhere for her to hide. Cameras and facial recognition are everywhere. Anywhere she goes she's going to leave a trail and anything I can't find myself, I have connections.

She's mine. I'm not going to let her run off and forget that. Run off and pretend like I don't exist, like I was just some fever dream she experienced for a few weeks before going back to her real life.

I throw the door open and my eyes go wide at the horror unfolding before me.

"Help." Riley slurs softly, more to the world than to me specifically, I don't think she's seen me yet. "Help, help, help." She cries, despair rolling down her face as Dubois pins my fiance up against a wall.

So much for that fucker not having to die.

I grab my gun off my back and cock it. Dubois turns as the sound resonates through the alley. "Get off of her." My rage instantly getting redirected. If I was acting feral before I'm sure there's no fucking way to describe me right now.

Oddly, I find myself slightly relieved. Riley didn't try to run. But now that my anger is no longer directed at her or Gia, I have no limits on unleashing it. And this asshole is about to know the full extent of my rage.

He looks to me and holds his hand up, taking a couple steps away from Riley. "This is a misunderstanding." He chuckles. "One I'm sure cash could clear up."

I scoff. "I don't think so."

Riley drops to the ground panting and curling into herself. She stares up at me with wide eyes. "Thank gods." She breathes heavily.

I yank the knife out of my boot, knowing my gun will probably be heard by everyone in the fucking bar. There are no cameras in this alley, I know that from watching it for the past week and I have a feeling Dubois knows that too, that's probably why he took Riley back here. It makes me wonder how many women he's done this too before.

I lunge at him, tackling him to the ground as I jab out at him with the knife, not really thinking all that much about actually being accurate and more just stabbing him because it will make me feel better. We go falling to the ground with my knife shoved into his chest.

He cries out in pain and I pull my knife back out. I cut across his throat and his sounds become garbled as blood starts to trickle down the sides of his neck and onto the ground. But I'm not done because I reel back and punch his dying body across the face as hard as I fucking can so that a snap and a crack resonate through the alley.

Riley gasps, and out of the corner of my eye I see her scrambling away from me towards the corner of the alley. She's stuck between me and the street though so I'm not worried about her trying to run off *now*.

I spit at Dubois face and know that's against every rule I ever learned about not leaving any trace of yourself, but I can't bring myself to care in this moment. I move backwards and stab my knife through his chest a few more times, just for good measure, but he's already dead.

Once I start to cool down I clean the knife off on the least bloody parts of Dubois's shirt and tuck it back into my boot before going to check on Riley.

She's still huddled in the corner looking at me with wide fearful eyes as I prowl towards her. She's shaking and I don't know if that's because of what she just saw me do, or because of what happened with Dubois.

"What happened?" I ask her, crouching down as close to her level as I can get. I want to brush the hair out of her face and kiss her tears away, but I don't touch her because I don't know what headspace she is in and if that would just make things worse.

Riley sniffles. "He... He slipped something in my drink." She mutters, her words coming out soft and slurred. Her eyes are glossy and she looks out of it. "I realized when I was in the bathroom and was going to go get Gia, but..." She looks over to the dead man and I can fill in the blanks.

I have half a mind to cut off the fucker's limp dick, but I think seeing that would just traumatize Riley further and she's been through enough for one night.

"Liam." She cries. "I'm so sorry."

I shake my head. "You have nothing to be sorry for, love. This wasn't your fault." I promise her, moving to stand. "Let me help you up. We need to get out of here." I grab her hand and she lets me pull her to her feet. "Keep your head down, Riley."

There's no time or means for me to dispose of Dubois, had I been more calculated maybe, but this wasn't work, this was a crime of passion. We're just going to have to leave his body for someone else to find and hope that there's not enough evidence behind for anyone to connect it to me.

She's shaking as I guide her out of the alley, wrapping an arm around her and pulling her into me. She has her gaze downcast as we rush into the streets and start walking back towards the hotel.

I pull out my phone and call Gabriel.

"Where the hell are you?" He growls.

"Are you still at the bar?" I ignore his question instead countering with one of my own.

"Yeah." He says. "Why?"

"Eyes down, Riley." I tell her as she glances up to look at me before turning my attention back to Gabriel. "Leave now. And out the front door. Don't go out the back."

He sighs. "What did you do?"

"I'll tell you when we get back to the hotel, but we need to leave Paris, tonight." I push Riley's head down. "Stop looking up at me. I don't want our faces to get caught on any of the cameras."

She nods and pushes herself further into my side, her body still trembling as we walk through the streets, getting closer to the hotel.

"Oh god." Gabriel says exasperatedly. "Alright, Gia and I will be there in a minute." He ends the call and I keep pulling Riley along.

It takes a while to get back to the hotel and when we finally get inside the suite, Riley promptly collapses onto the couch and starts crying. I let her, because I know she needs to get it out.

"Breathe, Riley." I rub her back softly and she curls herself into me.

She lets out a sob into my chest. "I was so fucking scared." She whimpers. "I..." She mutters.

I hush her softly. "I've got you, Riley." I promise her, I do run a hand through her hair then and tilt her chin to look at me. "I will always come find you, Riley. I'll never let anyone hurt you."

Riley looks up at me with wide red eyes. "You killed him." She whispers.

I nod.

"Good." She mutters.

I'm more than a little relieved that she says that. I knew it was likely she would see me kill someone at some point, but I was nervous how she would react. Maybe it's the shock or that she's angry at Dubois too, but she's not freaked out by what I did and I'll take that win after what just happened.

Riley and I stay there a while longer with me holding her until Gabriel and Gianna come through the door.

"What the fuck happened?" Gabriel asks gruffly. "Gia, go pack our stuff." And surprisingly she listens.

"Dubois was trying to assault Riley." I tell him.

Gabriel nods, instantly knowing how I would handle stumbling onto the situation without me even having to say anything else. "I'll go get the cars. We can leave in an hour, hopefully she'll be able to calm down by then." He then disappears back out the door.

Riley clings to me as I take her to go pack our stuff. After a few minutes of her laying down on the bed she goes quiet.

I sit down next to her. "Riley." I whisper softly.

She shakes her head.

"Riley." I repeat.

Her eyes are distant, staring off through the window at the Eiffel tower more like she's looking through it than at it. "I don't think I like Paris."

I chuckle softly. "Then let's get the hell out of here."

Chapter Twenty Four

Riley

We've been driving for about three hours. Liam keeps telling me to go to sleep, keeps telling me I'll feel better when I wake back up but I don't want to sleep right now. Instead I stare out the front windshield curled up in the passenger seat of the sports car with the blanket that Liam stole from the hotel.

Gianna and Gabriel are in the other car in front of us. Apparently we are making a stop in Venice before going back to New York and my whirlwind of a European trip ends.

I'm more than a little worried that this was just a wild vacation romance. What if we get back home and I realize just how big of a mistake I made by not running from him? What if this is all just lust, not love? What if when we go back to our real lives the honeymoon phase wears off and everything we built changes? What if he's too good to be true?

Maybe I'm overthinking it. I hope I'm overthinking it. But I've spent the entire time in this car just hoping that Liam will stay the passionate man who was willing to kill for me at the drop of a hat when we are back in Manhattan.

I glance over at him, his eyes locked on the road. His grip on the steering wheel is tight, like he's still upset about what happened earlier tonight. His eyes haven't calmed down yet either. There's something behind them I can't quite explain but it looks like a mix between a high and a need to scream.

I probably should be more upset about what happened with the man, who I've learned now was named Dubois. I should probably be caving in on myself and losing my mind, but I'm not. I've... I've been through worse. I've had it actually happen. A close call just spikes the adrenaline.

Intermittently my mind keeps flashing with images of the old bastard pressed against me, thoughts of the liquor on his breath as he tried to kiss me. He didn't get a kiss or to touch much more than my waist. Liam came fast enough that I was spared from having my body violated, just my mind.

I need a distraction.

My hand drifts across the small console between us and into my hero's lap. My fingers rub up and down on the legs of Liam's jeans before moving to his button and zipper.

"What are you doing?" He asks, his voice gruff.

"Thanking my savior for rescuing me." I purr, sliding the zipper down. The sound fills the car and everything goes silent for a second before I take his cock out of his boxers.

Liam shakes his head. "Riley, this seems like a bad idea." He keeps looking at the road though, not at me. We're on the highway and I see the speed at about one hundred kilometers per hour, I have no idea what that translates to in *miles* per hour which is what I have a frame of reference for, but I know it's decently fast based on how things are moving out the window.

"I don't care." I tell him, starting to slide my hand over his shaft.

"Riley." He growls, his voice a low warning. "You're not thinking clearly. You're acting out because you feel helpless. You shouldn't do this." I don't know if he's trying to convince himself or me.

"Do you not want me to do this?" I ask, pausing my hand to check that *he's* in the headspace for this.

Liam shakes his head. "I definitely didn't say that." My hand starts again before he can even get the next sentence out. "I want you always, Riley. I just don't want you confusing yourself. I don't want you to associate me with all the other traumatic men who have hurt you."

I shake my head. "I won't." I promise him. "I love you, Liam. I want you. I *need* you." He groans at that and I don't know if it's because of what I'm doing with my hand or my words. "I know you're different. You'll take care of me. I know that."

He nods. "Riley." His voice is gravely but full of the same need I feel coursing through me. Liam's cock is hard as a rock as I run my hand up and down him. His eyes are on the road, but I can see in them how distracted he is. I can see the way his attention wants to slip to me.

"Lean back." I tell him softly and he listens. I slip the belt over my chest behind my back and drop my head into his lap. I wrap my lips around his tip and start to suck, not holding back. I savor the taste of his cock and the sweat on his skin.

Liam lets out a gruff chuckle. "Oh, you are *definitely* acting out." He moans as I sink down fully onto him. I'm about to pull back up but one of his hands comes off the steering wheel to push down on my head. "Suck, love." He orders and I do. "That feels so fucking good."

My eyes water from how deep I'm taking him in my throat and a whimper slips free from my mouth, but I keep sucking because I love the way his abs are starting to twitch. I slip a hand between my own legs, under the blanket, and up my skirt, running two fingers up and down my pussy trying to calm some of my aching need.

He wraps his hand in my hair and starts to drag my head up and down his cock. "Fuck, Riley." I hear the car rev as he lets go of my head.

As I start to bob up and down on him, I notice him move into the fast lane. My eyes drift to the speedometer and I see the number climbing. My heart races, but I trust Liam, for some stupid reason, so I just keep going on his cock, letting him control the car and the world around us.

I rub at my own clit with one hand as I work the base of his cock with the other. I stroke up and down him, my lips staying around his tip, licking in circles around his head.

"Hold up your middle finger in the window on your side." Liam tells me.

I pull off of him. "What?"

Liam pushes me back down onto his dick. "We're passing Gabriel and Gia."

I laugh around his cock and flip them off, sure that they can see about where my head is positioned right now. Gia is definitely going to want to talk about this later.

"Good girl." Liam purrs and I can feel his arm that was on my head raise up and sit next to mine, likely flipping them off too. I hear a car rev that's not ours and Liam chuckles. "Head up, love, I think we're in a race and I need all my blood flow for that."

I pull my head off his cock and glance over to see Gabriel and Gia's car rushing ahead of us on the empty road. Stars and a few street lights are all that illuminate the highway as Liam slams down on the pedal and the car speeds up.

I gasp, grabbing the seat and feeling the push back as the car begins to pass theirs. I glance over at the speedometer and see we're pushing two hundred. "How... how fast is that?" I mutter out.

"About one twenty five in miles per hour." He smirks, his hands firm on the wheel.

I'm definitely out of my head now because all I can do is feel the fear overtaking me. My head kicks back and I look up through the sunroof to see the stars as we scream past. Intermittently signs pass overhead so fast I can't have any hope of making them out even if I spoke the language on them.

"This is insane." I whisper, barely audible over the roar of the engine.

"You like a little crazy though, love." Liam purrs and I see the speedometer climb up another ten numbers. His phone starts ringing in the cupholder. "Answer it."

I pick it up and see Gianna across the top. I slide it open and hear a laugh from her come through the line.

"Think you're real cool, don't you?" Gabriel huffs through the line.

Liam shrugs even though Gabriel can't see it. "I did just have my fiancee's head in my lap while going about ninety so, yeah." He chuckles. "I think that makes me pretty fucking cool."

Gabriel scoffs through the phone. "I'll race you twenty miles."

"I thought you were already trying to race me." Liam glances in the rearview briefly. "And losing. Badly."

Gabriel just says, "Twenty miles."

"What do I get when I win?" Liam asks.

I can *hear* Gianna roll her eyes. "Men, always have to turn everything into a competition." She sighs and I laugh.

"I'll buy you a jet." Gabriel says.

My eyes go wide and so do Liam's. "Seriously?" He asks.

"A small one!" Gabriel corrects quickly. "But if I win I want you to start coming on jobs from now on. I'm tired of always having to take Dante when I need a second."

"Deal." Liam huffs a laugh. "Better start thinking of jet names, love. Looks like we won't have to fly commercial on our honey-moon."

Gabriel growls through the phone and then I see his car start to speed up behind us.

"Do you think we can name our jet Bob?" I suggest with a giggle.

Liam glares at me softly. "Absolutely fuck-ing not." He tells me, quickly turning his at-tention back to the road. "Come up with some-thing better."

I cross my arms over my chest. "I like the name Bob." I mutter as I watch Gabriel try to overtake us.

"No." Liam answers simply. He pushes the pedal all the way down and I don't bother look-ing at the speedometer anymore, but I don't think I want to know how fast we are going.

"I'm going to win!" Gabriel says through the phone.

"Riley?" Liam says.

"Yeah?" I reply.

"Hang up." He tells me gruffly.

I do as I'm told and slip the phone back into the cup holder. I make note of the mile mark-er we are on and watch as they start flying past us faster than I can really comprehend. The world blurs outside the window and the only thing even close to keeping up with us is Gabriel and Gia. With how late it is there's no one out and that allows them to enable their little race.

A turn comes up around the bend and as we glide through it Gabriel starts to get close to passing us. For a split second I think he will and then he... he slows down? I get confused until I look over, seeing the way Gia is leaning into him in a position I was just in a few minutes ago and realize exactly *why* Gabriel had to slow down.

We lose him quickly after that since apparently Gia decided to throw for the other team. As we cruise past the mile marker for what will be eighteen I tell Liam. "You better thank Gianna for that jet."

He chuckles. "Did she do what I think she did?"

I nod. "Yup."

"I owe her one." Liam holds the car steady as we continue to soar down the dark road.

"You still owe *me* one." I correct him. "Given a very different one than you owe Gianna now." I chew on my lip a little.

A very short amount of time passes before we soar past the mile marker for twenty past where we started, but once we're on the other side Liam starts to slow down and pulls off on the shoulder. He picks up his phone and it rings for a second before Gabriel answers.

"I want a rematch!" He argues.

"No." Liam huffs a laugh as he starts to scoot his chair back. "I expect my jet by the end of the month. Thanks Gianna!"

"Can't have my best friend flying commercial." She makes a shuddering sound.

Liam grabs me by the waist and I shriek as he pulls me over the console and onto his lap, the blanket flying off in the process. He starts undoing his pants with his free hand. "I gotta go. I'll see you in Venice."

"Bastard." Gabriel grumbles as the phone call ends.

Liam reaches up under my skirt and rips my panties off of me. I feel them seperate from my skin with a sharp sting everywhere the fabric tried to hold on. He pulls it free and brings them to his face, taking a deep whiff and sighing happily. "Fuck, you smell divine."

My eyes go wide. "Liam." I whisper.

He lifts me up and I know I'm soaked as he lowers me down onto his cock. He lets out a groan and I respond in turn. He starts to work my hips on him as much as he can in the cramped space of the car.

My head is so close to hitting the ceiling, but I don't even fucking care. I lean down into him, pressing my lips to his with reckless abandon. I don't know if it's the adrenaline or the sense of victory or what ever fucking else, but kissing him has never felt better.

Euphoria overtakes me as he lays his seat back as far as it will go. I grind my hips into him, leaning down so my chest is pressed into his. Our bodies push and pull rhythmically against each other in a way that feels so right. In a way that makes me question how I ever lived without him.

His hand runs through my hair before slowly drifting down the side of my face and wrapping around my throat. He holds me like that and uses his grip to move my body up and down on him faster.

I start to feel a little lightheaded, my face flushing as I try desperately to suck in oxygen and can't. I start to struggle, reaching up to grab at his hand but he grabs both of mine with his free one and pins them between the two of us.

"Don't fight, Riley." He purrs.

I whimper, feeling that fear slice through me as stars dance around the corners of my vision. "Please, Sir." I choke out my plea.

He thrusts up into me and loosens his hold just slightly but doesn't let go. Liam keeps us moving in a way that I have absolutely no hope of helping with because of how clouded my head is right now. "Fuck, you feel so good, love." And then his cock slams into me in a way that has my eyes rolling into the back of my head.

Yeah, this man has me all sorts of fucked up and I think I like it. I think I *love* it. I need him more than the oxygen he's depriving me from. I'm pretty sure I would give this man anything he ever fucking asked of me just to have the ability to touch him for a single second.

Is this what love feels like or is this obsession? I feel fucking insane but he said we could be insane together. I want to be insane together.

His hand finally lets go of my neck and I suck down a gasping breath, my body falling down onto his chest with him no longer holding me up. He keeps fucking me through it though, his hands going to my hips now and rolling them into him. His fingers dig into me and I let out a soft cry.

"Fuck." I moan. "Liam."

"Riley." He responds, his breath catching seconds before he groans and I feel him release into me. He seats me fully onto him as he finishes and when he's done he picks me up off his cock.

Liam pushes me back against the steering wheel and a honk sounds from the car when I lean against it causing me to jump. He chuckles before his hand drifts between the two of us, his fingers starting to work my clit.

My breath saws in and out of my lungs as he drags his fingers down, dipping them into me before his thumb finds the bundle of nerves at my center. I grind my pelvis into his hand and my eyes roll back in my head.

"I think you said I owed you something, Riley." Liam purrs. "I always pay my debts, love." His pressure increases and I'm already so tender from how hard he was just fucking and choking me.

I nod emphatically and can't help myself from starting to beg. "Yes, Sir, please." My lips fall open on a pant. "I swear to the gods if you don't give me an orgasm this time I'm going to be the one putting the gun in your mouth."

Liam chuckles. "You're never going to let that go are you?"

I shake my head. "Nope."

He leans into me. "Then maybe I will just have to make you forget." He curls his fingers inside of me and his thumb flicks over my center in a way that has me twitching. "Cum for me, Riley."

My back presses into the steering wheel behind me as he lures me over the edge. After another minute of him working me I feel myself clench, my body tensing as the orgasm starts to ride through me. I scream out as I finish, crumpling into a heap in his lap.

"That's a good girl." He smiles and it's the best sight in the entire world.

Chapter Twenty Five

Liam

Gabriel and I pull up at Luigi's house in Venice with the two sports cars we had to drive eleven fucking hours. It took us roughly all day, but we were able to power through. I even let Riley drive for a little while. She opened up the car way more than I was fucking expecting, it was badass as hell and just reminded me how much I love her.

She got really fucking nervous when I stuck my hand between her legs, it was fucking adorable. Watching her try to concentrate on the road, chewing on her lip and her eyes wide was one of the best sights of this whole trip.

"Ah, you found my cars." Luigi smiles.

"Anything to help family." Gabriel says. "It was really no problem. They were just sitting around in Paris. I wouldn't take them back there anytime soon."

Luigi nods knowingly. "That can be arranged. Nico." He waves his son over to the cars that we were climbing out of. "Take these back to the garage for me."

Gabriel and I dropped Riley and Gianna at the airport earlier today before we brought the cars to Luigi's. They don't need to be at these kinds of meetings and I know Riley will wait for me to get back.

After hearing her call me her savior, which definitely gave me a fucking complex by the way, I knew the trauma bond was strong enough that she has no intention of leaving me. Now she sees me as the man who rescued her from an alley in Paris, not the man who took her at the airport in New York.

Nico starts examining the cars, looking for what I don't know and probably never will. There was some reason these cars were so valuable, but whatever that reason was, isn't any of our business, as Gabriel keeps reiterating to me.

"Come in. Let's have dinner before you go back home." Luigi waves us into the ornate home. They are on the canal, the salmon colored stone house stretching up four stories with rounded windows. It isn't as big as their home in Sicily, but I'm sure the view more than makes up for it.

They don't really care that much about dinner, they want to make sure whatever they had in those cars is still there before we leave. It should be, I doubt Monreaux and Corbin were smart enough to search them and I'm sure the Duboises didn't care to.

I had told Gabriel *we* should look for whatever was hidden in them, not to take it but just so we knew exactly what we were involved in. Gabriel told me it was more important to mind our business so my curiosity will sadly not get satiated.

Luigi leads up through the home into the dining room that faces out onto the water, which is almost turquoise in the setting sun. There are a few boats lining the sides but none of them are moving, everything is so still.

The walls of the dining room are a soft cream going up into arched vaulted ceilings. The floor to ceiling windows have tan curtains draped off to the side of them and line the back and left walls of the room.

The table here is larger than the one back in Sicily, likely because they do more business in Venice. The chairs are a dark colored wood with leather seat covers. A matching buffet table sits to the wall on the right of the room with several bottles of liquor and wine on them, at least two of which were the same bottles of whiskey from our last meeting.

Luigi moves over to the table and picks up the bottle of whiskey. He pours three glasses, passing one to Gabriel and then to me. "To my cars."

"Salute." Gabriel nods softly.

"Salute." I repeat before taking a sip of the perfect whiskey and trying to take a peek at the bottle so I can get some later. This would be a good gift for Gabriel's birthday.

Luigi gestures over to the table. "Please sit." He pulls out the seat at the head and Gabriel takes the one beside him across from the water. "Did you have any trouble in Paris?" He asks, and I'm sure he already knows the answer to that question.

Dubois was a big enough name that his death made headlines. No one found any footage of me from the scene. Riley and I had been able to avoid the cameras walking away and there wasn't one facing that alley. My spit got picked up, but according to the police records they weren't able to match it.

The bar cameras were not working that night for some reason the police can't figure out. I had disabled them before Gabriel and I had gone to get the cars, more for the ones in the parking garage, but I had luckily gotten the bar cameras too. So there was no record of anyone who went in or out that night.

The bartender and a few of the patrons gave a shaky description of a tall angry man with tattoos who went out the back, but their sketches of me all suck unless you know who you're looking at. Luigi knew who he was looking at.

"None we couldn't handle." Gabriel answers.

Luigi nods but he seems skeptical. "I'm sure you gentlemen will be back in the states soon enough anyways." His way of telling us to get the fuck out of Europe before we caused any problems for him.

This is my fault. What I did with Dubois was far from professional. I should have pulled him off Riley and killed him later that night in a more secure location but when I caught sight of him touching her all I saw was red.

"We leave tonight." Gabriel assured him.

"I'm sure that's for the best." Luigi said.

"Been away from the kids for too long anyways. They are old enough where they do okay on their own, but the wife worries." Gabriel takes a slow sip of his whiskey, his eyes watching Luigi carefully.

Luigi nods. "No matter how old, your children will always be your children. I know Nico will always be my boy, even with him now more than a man."

As if he could hear us talking about him, Nico comes through the door. "I got the cars put away in the garage." He says with a gruff nod.

"How are my cars?" Luigi asks Nico.

"As they should be." He responds.

I can tell Gabriel is relieved hearing that, but he doesn't show it on his face. He just takes another sip of his whiskey and smiles. "We help our family." Gabriel promises.

"I'm sure we can help you too, in the future." Luigi smiles back.

Gabriel raises his glass. "To the future."

Chapter Twenty Six

Riley

The trip back to Manhattan was mostly pretty boring although Liam and I did have sex on the plane again, just to make *sure* we are a part of the mile high club because Liam claimed he *wasn't sure we did it right the first time.* Gianna laughed when I came out of the bathroom pulling down my skirt and Gabriel just sighed.

It was weird not going back to my own apartment. Liam's penthouse is in a very different part of New York than I was in. Everything is so posh here. It's beyond fancy and I don't think I'll have any trouble finding a nice new bar to go write in on days where the quiet of home isn't doing it for me.

Home... This is my home now, because home is wherever Liam is. And that feels so crazy, but I never want to be apart from him. I know if I have him, I'm safe. He'll keep me safe.

The silver elevator carries us upwards and I feel a weird sense of nerves I can't quite explain. Going back to real life is going to be odd. I'm scared, but I trust Liam. He's always taken care of me and I know he'll keep doing that, location shouldn't matter. But then why can't I calm the jitters in my stomach.

Liam takes the bag out of my hands and sets it down in the elevator. He grabs me, picking me up and cradling me in his arms.

I laugh. "What the fuck are you doing?"

"Carrying you over the threshold." He says as the elevator door opens and he walks us through it before setting me down and getting our bags.

I roll my eyes. "We aren't married yet."

He sets the bags down on the sparkling black floors and pushes me up against the soft blue wall so fast I almost can't even take in the view of the floor to ceiling windows that seem to take up the entire front of the room.

Liam's hand goes to my hip as his lips find my neck starting to suck on the soft tender skin there. It has been at least a couple days since he gave me a hickey, I'm overdue. I've more than noticed how he loves to mark his territory. He clamps down and my eyes close as I grind my body into him. He can mark me any time he wants.

"We can get married sooner if you can't wait til June to have my last name." He purrs as he pulls away from the red raised skin.

My stomach sinks a little. "June." I say, like a soft plea. "I think any sooner and I might still bolt." I tell him honestly.

Liam chuckles. "You won't get far." He promises and for some reason it's more of a comfort than a threat. "I'm not taking the anklet off until I have to replace it."

I nod. "I think I'm okay with that." The anklet was how he was able to find me, able to save me. I can live with a little bit of added surveillance knowing that the person watching me will always come to my rescue when I need them.

"Good." Liam presses a kiss to my forehead. He pulls away from me and I finally get a good look of his living room, *our* living room.

There are spotless plush white couches placed in front of the windows so they look out onto the city. A few softly colored wooden end tables sit near the couches and have different random things on them like coasters and one of my books that looks rather worn. A soft light gray shaggy carpet sits beneath them and it looks like it would feel so fucking good on my back. I have a feeling I'll find that out at some point.

The ceiling stretches high and there are stairs off to the side that have a glass banister and a railing that go up to the second floor. This place is way bigger than my tiny apartment.

I turn slowly, my heels clicking softly on the dark floors and see the kitchen in the back of the space. The white cabinets and marble counter tops look pristine, but I guess no one has been here in almost a month at this point.

The only thing not perfect in the space is the many stacks of brown boxes off to the side labeled miscellaneously, but all sharing one similar tag, *Riley*. I walk over to the boxes, my hand skirting over the cardboard as I get lost in thought.

My entire life got packed up into this and dragged here. I feel Liam come up behind me, his hand resting on the small of my back.

"Too much all at once, love?" He asks, brushing some of the hair from my face.

I shrug. "Maybe." I say, but then my eyes glance out the window again. "But was there ever another option?" I ask softly.

"No." He replies.

"A lot of people don't get to choose the life they live and theirs aren't nearly as beautiful as this." I stare at the buildings and the stars spotting the night sky. The constellations seem to shimmer at me and I'm almost surprised they are even visible. In my apartment I could never see them. There were a lot of things I never saw before Liam.

"Do you want to unpack?" He asks. Despite how late it is we are both pretty awake right now. "Maybe it will make you feel more at home to put some of your stuff away."

I shake my head. "In the morning." I tell him.

Liam nods. He moves away from me and goes to his laptop bag. He pulls out my phone and hands it to me.

I take it gingerly, more than a little surprised. "You're giving me it back?" I ask, a part of me thought he was going to keep it forever.

"You'll need it. Your editor is pissed you haven't responded to any of the corrections she's made and Anna has been very concerned why you disappeared for a few weeks." Liam says and I just kind of stare at him. "I want you to have your own life, Riley. I just want that life to be intertwined with mine so fully you'll never have any hopes of separating us."

"Thank you." I whisper, sliding open the phone. I open up my camera and walk over to the windows. I position my ring in front of the skyline and stars to take a picture. I go to instagram and in the description I type, "When your book boyfriend comes to life." I tack on a few different hashtags before posting it.

Liam's phone goes off.

"You have alerts set up for my posts?" I ask.

He laughs. "You act like you don't know me." Liam hits a few things on his phone and smiles. "They are already in the comments."

"Really?" I pull my phone back out. I have comment notifications and likes turned off because of just how many I get.

GIRL, YOU DISAPPEAR AND SHOW BACK UP WITH A MAN AND YOU WON'T EVEN DO A FACE REVEAL!?! WHAT THE ABSOLUTE HELL??? Followed by a few angry emojis and a *But seriously so happy for you.* And then some hearts.

OMG!!! He did so good! Look at that view! Lucky man! With more hearts and ring emojis.

I had no idea you were even dating anyone! Congrats! This one had heart eyes after it.

And the comment that stood out the most. An anonymous account with no face, no profile, no nothing that posted one word. *Mine.* Followed by a devil smirking emoji.

I glance up at Liam knowing exactly who that account belongs to. I click on the comment and reply. *So possessive.* Immediately after I do both mine and his comment start getting a ton of likes.

"Can I have Gianna's number?" I ask him, passing him my phone knowing he'll give it back.

Liam smiles as he takes it. He punches in one contact then another. "Mine is already in there under *Husband,* I just put in Gabriel and Gianna's."

I huff a laugh. "I really hope I never need Gabriel's."

Liam chuckles. "In case of emergency." He shrugs.

I shoot off a quick text to Gianna. *It's Riley. Liam gave me my phone back.*

Her reply is instant. *Good it will be so much easier to drag you out shopping when I have your number. Speaking of which, let's get drinks tomorrow.*

Liam grabs me around the waist and my phone is no longer what I'm paying attention to. All I can focus on are his green eyes staring into me like I'm the only thing in the world that he sees.

In that moment the life I'm going to build with him doesn't seem that scary. It feels natural. It feels like what I've been missing and just never knew it. And I realize that I have never known someone who makes me feel so at home.

"I love you, Riley."

"I love you too, Liam."

"No I think this time?" He chuckles.

I shake my head. "No. This time I know."

Epilogue

Liam

The brown wooden barn upstate is a way bigger venue than needed for the very few of us
at our wedding, but it was what Riley wanted.
We looked at a few different wedding venues
since Riley insisted she didn't want to get married in our living room or in Gabriel's backyard.

It's a nice backyard, Gianna spent thou-
sands on it, I thought it was fine. Riley said no.
But to be fair to Riley I would marry her in a
sewer if there were no better options. I don't
care where we get married as long as she's the
one I'm marrying.

Today my suit doesn't feel so uncomfortable.
I no longer feel annoyed and strangled by having to wear a tie. For her I'll wear it happily.

The high beams, arches, and support poles are covered in green and white florals all wrapped around carefully by the florists who demanded way too much money to loop flowers around something. Weddings are a racket, especially when you plan one on six months notice. We had to buy multiple vendors out from other people, people who were pissed but we have money and guns so they can fuck off.

Sunlight and rain stream in from between the slats and in the holes of the barn roof, little droplets falling down into the space. This barn is the original that was built, some number of years ago that I don't remember being told but was a lot. The property has a reception hall and other places to get married that wouldn't result in us getting sprinkled with rain, but Riley liked the barn so I did too. Besides I hear rain on your wedding day is good luck.

The property used to be farmland but has since been renovated into a wedding venue which we of course bought out all of even with it just being the two of us, Gabriel, Gianna, and their kids. Sofia, Enzo, and Bella rather like their new aunt Riley, more than me and I'm almost offended considering I've known all of them since birth. But regardless they wanted to be here to see us get married.

I take a deep breath trying to center myself but there's something about standing at the end of the aisle that's just nerve racking in a way that I haven't felt since I proposed. My mind is racing and I'd be lying if I said I wasn't at least a little concerned about Riley getting cold feet.

The last few months have been amazing and not just the sex either. We've had so many days staying up til two in the morning talking and cuddling in the living room. Staring out at the stars with deep conversations is a lot more fun than I was expecting, especially with Riley. There have been mornings filled with coffee and work over the breakfast table, looking up and seeing her smiling at me makes it so much better than working alone.

We've been happy and I know she's happy because she's told me as much. But still, a part of her will always remember what I did to get her and I don't want that part of Riley reminding her that white fluttering gowns look very pretty running away.

After today I won't have to worry about it. She'll truly be mine. She'll have promised as much in front of me and god *and her gods* (don't get me started we've had multiple arguments already about what religious beliefs we're raising our kids with. She'll win, but I'm still going to at least try. I'm not all that religious anyways, who cares. Besides the only god she truly needs to believe in is *me*, the rest she can do what she wants with).

I've been waiting for all of thirty seconds but I already want to check the damned tracker on her because I haven't seen her since last night. She stayed with Gabriel and Gianna because of some stupid superstition about not being able to see the bride before the wedding. I kept rolling over in the night and trying to pull her into my arms only to keep realizing she wasn't there. I slept like crap, probably part of why I'm so irritable.

The doors open at the end of the barn and Riley is standing there in the most beautiful white gown I've ever seen in my life. It's simple, understated, *her*. It's perfect, she's perfect.

Her eyes are wide behind her glasses as she takes in the space before her, her bare feet under the dress standing on the pavers right outside the barn. She wanted to not wear shoes, something about feeling in touch with the world around her when she got married? I didn't really understand it, but I just nodded and told her it was whatever she wanted.

That was part of the reason she liked the barn on the back of the property instead of one of the more modern options. The floors were still made of dirt and had never gotten properly done, something about the aesthetic and that was why we had to pay three times the price for the option without finished flooring. Like I said, weddings are a racket. Riley loved it however so that makes it perfect.

I see her take a deep breath before starting to make her way towards me without an ounce of hesitation in her steps. I know Paris was a turning point, but I never expected this much of a change. She's been more sure of our relationship than I was expecting and it has been putting me more at ease, albeit not fully.

Riley pads down the aisle towards me, the nerves on her face likely as obvious as the ones on mine but she doesn't stop, doesn't take her eyes off me, she keeps walking. Her bouquet of white roses is beautiful in her shaking hands, she passes it off to Gianna who smiles at her as Riley moves to stand next to me.

"Fancy seeing you here." She whispers softly, chuckling at her own joke, likely trying to soothe some of her nerves.

"You look incredible, Riley." I smile at her.

She blushes. "Thanks. You clean up pretty nice yourself." Riley runs a hand through her blonde hair, likely more as a nervous tick than because she doesn't like the way it's sitting. She has it half up with a section twisted back to hold her veil and the rest curled neatly, falling around her in gentle waves.

Her makeup is soft and it reminds me of the first time we had sex. The way she did just a little bit to have it noticeable but not so much as to overpower her usual no makeup look.

If Riley wouldn't get mad at me I'd pin her against the wall and rip the dress off of her right fucking now. But Riley made it very *very* clear that if I ripped her wedding dress that there would be hell to pay, *even if I do understand how that could be sexy, I will slit your throat and then Gabriel will be very mad at me.*

I had just laughed and told her that I'd like to see her try, at which point she pulled out a butter knife and proceeded to attempt to chase me down with it, trying to prove her point.

She ended up pinned against a wall with me holding it to *her* neck and hopefully learned a very valuable lesson about who the fuck is in charge. But I won't rip the dress. I have a feeling she'd be a lot more passionate if she was actually trying to kill me.

The priestess that Riley chose starts to speak about love and unity and whatever other stereotypical stuff they say at weddings but all I can focus on is the soft scent of Riley's floral perfume intermingling with the light rain and freshly cut grass. I bet it would taste even better licked off her neck than it smells.

Apparently I'm fantasizing about licking the sweat off her skin for longer than I thought because everything goes by in a blur and the next thing I remember is the priestess saying my name.

"Liam, do you take Riley as your lawfully wedded wife-" She says a few more things that I thoroughly black out because I'm back to thinking about sucking on Riley, but I know the general premise so I reply.

"I do."

"Riley," The priestess pauses.

Riley immediately rushes out, "I do." Likely zoning out in similar ways to myself. Honestly, it was really cute.

The priestess chuckles, "Riley, I have to finish the declaration of intent first."

Riley's face is bright red as she shakes her head. "Right. Sorry."

"You're okay, love." I promise her. I'm just relieved she said *I do* at all. I don't really give a fuck that she did it at the wrong moment. The priestess however does, because she starts the declaration of intent again.

"Riley, do you take Liam to be your lawfully wedded husband? Do you promise to cherish and adore him, forsaking all others, and remaining true to him until your dying day?"

Riley nods. "I do."

Contrary to popular opinion in media, this is not the moment I got to kiss Riley. No, instead we had to exchange rings and then the priestess made us tie a very pretty piece of rope that I had seen Riley working on intermittently over the last couple weeks (I would have preferred it wrapped around her wrist in a different context). Somehow I did manage to make it through the ceremony and follow the minimal instructions from the priestess, while still fantasizing about fucking Riley up against the barn door.

Finally after what felt like a small eternity the priestess did say the words I had been waiting for since I saw the doors open and Riley standing at the entrance. "You may now kiss the bride."

"Thank fucking god." I grab Riley roughly around the waist and pull her into my body, feeling the silky white fabric under my fingertips. She chuckles softly as I take my hand and tilt her chin up to me. I press my lips to hers desperately wanting to drink in her being in a way that feels more spiritual than physical.

Riley moans into my lips, her body melting into my touch as I try with everything in me *not* to start stripping her bare on the spot. The dress is more than beautiful but I desperately want to see what's underneath it.

After a minute of me chewing on Riley the priestess clears her throat. We pull apart and there is a brief pause before the priestess says. "Well that was it. Usually there's a recessional, but there are all of like seven of you so, congratulations Mr. and Mrs. Mitchell."

"Thank you." Riley smiles softly, but I'm already starting to pull her away. She lets out a shrieking chuckle as I drag her back down the aisle.

I lean into her and purr in her ear. "Let's go find somewhere private."

Riley giddily follows behind me and her look of excitement has me fucking thrilled. The rest of our lives together can't start soon enough.

As I drag her out the doors of the barn and up towards the suites the venue gave us to get ready in, Riley whispers. "We can't have sex."

I turn to her. "Why?"

"I forgot my birth control when I went to Gabriel and Gianna's last night." She answers.

Stopping, I pull her into my arms and lean into her. "You didn't forget it, Riley." I whisper. "I took it out of your bag and threw it away."

Her eyes go wide. "Liam." She gasps softly.

"You don't need it anymore, Riley." I tell her softly, pressing a kiss to her lips before picking her up into my arms and carrying her towards the stairs to the bridal suite behind one of the other barns.

"Liam!" She objects. "You can't be serious."

I huff a laugh. "You should know your husband better than that, Riley." I smirk at her.

Riley seems like she's going to object again, but then I'm pressing my lips to hers and those objections fall silent.

I bring her up the stairs to the suite. The room is a pristine baby blue color with fluffy curtains covering the windows. There is a row of mirrors with a floor length one in the middle and counters on both sides of it. There are chairs to do makeup or hair or whatever else in as well as a few couches in a soft white color. The white marble floors are sparkling, from the way they were cleaned or glitter I'm not entirely sure.

The windows behind the mirror overlook the gardens and field on the property. There are bags and a bunch of random things strewn across the space, likely from Riley and the girls getting ready. The men's space down stairs was a lot more hardwood and leather as opposed to this light and fluffy room for the ladies.

I close and lock the door behind us as I push Riley into the room, her veil fluttering slightly with the movement. I prowl towards her, backing her up towards the counter and mirrors.

Riley's back hits against them and that's when she comes back to her senses. "Liam, I swear to the gods if you actually threw out my birth control, I am never going to let you fuck me again."

I huff a chuckle. "We both know that's not true, Riley." I purr and the way her steely expression falters just proves me right. "You don't need it anymore, Riley." I lean into her again and whisper in her ear. "You're going to look so beautiful pregnant with my baby."

The way she whimpers tells me she isn't totally against the idea. "I... Umm..." She mutters out, clearly beyond flustered as she tries to figure out how to react to what I said.

I brush her hair behind her ear, petting her softly as I start to pepper kisses to her neck and jaw. "Tell me you want that, Riley. Tell me to fuck you until you're so cum drunk you can't think straight."

She shudders. "Fuck, why do I want that?" She asks more of herself than me. "I shouldn't want that. I should be telling you no."

"We both know you've never been good at telling me no." I start to suck the soft flesh of her neck into my mouth and feel her body starting to tense beneath me.

"This is such a bad idea." Riley whispers, her head kicking back on a moan.

"Why?" I ask pulling away from her. She seems a little surprised that I stopped as the lust from her eyes starts to subside and give way into the serious discussion I'm trying to have. "We're married. Over twenty five. Financially stable. And in love. Why is it a bad idea for us to have kids?"

Riley chews on her lip for a second, seeming to need a moment to process. "Don't you think it's too soon? We just got married. Literally less than fifteen minutes ago. We've been together less than six months. I mean... What if we're making a mistake? What if you wake up in another six months and realize you rushed into things?"

"Are you scared I'm going to think that, or that you're going to think that?" I challenge softly.

Riley shrugs. "Either." She answers honestly. "What if... what if it's too good to be true?" She asks, casting her gaze down to her feet.

"Then I want to enjoy it for everything it has right now instead of worrying about what might not be later." I tilt her chin up to look at me. "I don't want to live our lives on the fear of regret. This version of me, Riley, I want to make a life with you. And I don't think we should let hypothetical future versions of ourselves decide differently. Especially when I know that this version of you, you want to make a life with me too."

She nods. "Yes." Riley whispers.

"Then let's make a life together."

Acknowledgements

Thank you to YOU, the reader! Without you I would just be screaming into the void. You make me not just a crazy person rambling into her computer screen for hours on end... okay maybe I'm still those things but with you read-ing I'm not doing so pointlessly so thank you.

Thank you to all my friends and family for supporting me both in my life and in my writing. I have an amazing support system that allows me to flourish and I am eternally grateful for that.

Thank you to Liam for being the intrusive thought that popped into my head one day going through the airport and inspired this whole cute little story. When I texted my best friend about the idea I never expected anything to actually come of it so I'm grateful that you had enough to say that I could make you a story.

Thank you to Riley for being the off brand version of myself that I wish I was. Ever just thought, what if this happened to me? And then wrote it? Gotta love a self insert, thanks girl for the adventure.

Thank you to my PA (Halla), my best friend (Tullie Summers), and my alpha reader (Nerdy), all who helped me develop this book and I can't thank the three of you enough for that. Because of you three I was able to take an idea and make it a reality and I always appreciate your support.

Thank you to all the authors who came before me and inspired my works. Nothing is ever original and I'm okay with that. Where have I heard that before?

As always, thank you to typos. Withoot you I would be nothing. You make me the author I am today and I love you.

Finally, I want to thank God, because God gave me this book, and I feel God in this Chili's tonight.

About the Author

I'm bad at talking about myself but can write a 500 page book about someone else. Do with that information what you will.

As a kid I dreamed of being an author. I took a creative writing class in high school then proceeded to go on with my life and do nothing with it. That was until one day I decided to open a silly little document and start writing a silly little story about a healer and two kings who were in love with her. That cute little pet project that I thought would just be scrapped ten chapters in turned into a full blown trilogy that I'm more proud of than I can even explain.

I've always been a dreamer and sometimes if you keep your head in the clouds long enough, you do actually touch the stars.

I got married in September of 2024 to my loving husband. We had been together 4 years at that point and he's always encouraged me to go after what I'm passionate in. Finding that person who helps you achieve is so important and it's the best quality trait I could ask for in a partner.

Thanks for spending your time to read this. I hope you're having a great day and please make sure to check out my works. There's always more coming out. I'm one of those people who always has to be working on something so I promise you I am.

Check Out My Other Works

<u>**The Asher Series**</u>
Asher
Burned
Change

Check Out My Socials

Tiktok: @84Lele
   Instagram: @the84Lele
   Twitter: @84Lele84Lele
   YouTube: @84Lele

www.ingramcontent.com/pod-product-compliance
Lightning Source LLC
Chambersburg PA
CBHW031202310726
48969CB00001B/182